The Liberation

Marissa Shrock

Cimelia Press

The Liberation

Published by Cimelia Press, Greentown, Indiana
Printed in the United States of America
ISBN-13: 978-0-9969879-0-5
Library of Congress Control Number: 2016901759

To Aunt Suzanne

Thank you for your love and support.

"For my thoughts are not your thoughts, neither are your ways my ways," declares the Lord. "As the heavens are higher than the earth, so are my ways higher than your ways, and my thoughts than your thoughts."

Isaiah 55:8-9

CHAPTER 1

There are always battles on the journey to a happy ending, and Emancipation Warriors Agent Jethro Portner was my first.

"You gotta know, Miss Wilkins, that 'cause of your background, I ain't thrilled about having you at my training camp." Jethro's gunmetal eyes stared me down and made me thankful his spotless desk provided a barrier between us.

After all the information I'd supplied his organization because of my hacking, he should be ecstatic, but I bit my tongue and met his gaze. How old was he? At least forty judging from his bald spot and the white hairs that frosted his sideburns. A gold chain embellished his neck, and a snake tattoo curled around his forearm and bicep.

My skin crawled.

Jethro chomped a wad of gum before continuing in his gravelly voice. "However, Agent Freeman recommends you, and since he's one of our best, I'm trusting him. It don't hurt you got information that'll clear the Warriors of involvement in President Hernandez's assassination."

"And the attempt on my mother's life."

"Right." Jethro's chair screeched. "'Nough about that. I got stuff we need to discuss."

"Okay." Being cooperative would get me out of here faster, so I could fight in the revolution against the United Regions of North America's corrupt government.

"You need a new alias. Your first got blown. Now you'll be twenty-three-year-old Fredrica Lloyd."

I nodded. The name sounded cool.

"Second, you gotta understand the objective of this camp." Jethro cleared his throat. "It ain't preparing folks for combat or restoration. We train for liberation."

"Of prisoners?"

"Right. The government stuck so many citizens in prison under that ridiculous Peace and Unity Act that we gotta have lots of liberation agents. It's one of the Warriors' most dangerous assignments." Jethro extended his palm. "Gimme your courier."

"Why?" I clutched the device the Warriors used to communicate securely with each other without the government knowing.

He bristled. "If you're gonna stay here, you gotta obey orders. Without explanation."

I slapped it into his palm. Jethro rested his courier on top of mine. A few seconds later, he returned it. "There's a schedule and a dossier for your new identity. Read it. Memorize it. Destroy it. Don't be late for training tomorrow morning."

I started to stand.

"Sit." His bicep twitched, causing the snake to appear as if it were snatching prey. "Never leave 'til you're dismissed. Got it?"

"Yes sir." My face grew warm.

"I'd better see you following rules. Like everyone else."

I told myself the less trouble I caused, the faster I could graduate and help Ben.

"If you wanna be an agent, then you gotta impress me." Jethro smirked. "I get the final decision on whether or not you get outta camp. And how soon."

Judging from his expression, I might never leave.

"I told ya how I feel about you being here. You got attitude. You're young. You gotta have stuff your way." He paused and leaned back in his chair. "You think the time you spent hiding out playing hacker and that rogue mission with Ben Lagarde qualify you for agent status."

I didn't, but he seemed pretty confident in his ability as a mind reader. I raised my eyebrows.

"They don't." Jethro's eyes grew icy. "Got it?"

"Yes sir."

He gripped the edge of his desk. "Time for a polygraph." He stood. "Let's go."

* * *

Jethro led me to a small room dominated by a metal and glass tube. His hand flicked an impatient wave toward the machine, and he took a seat behind a desk. The tube's door yawned, and I shuffled inside. Two orange footprints adorned the rubber-coated floor, so I moved my feet into place, facing Jethro. To my left was a mirror on the wall. I examined it. Was someone else watching?

"Nobody's back there," Jethro said.

The tube's glass door hissed closed, encasing me. Two light beams, one red and one blue, pierced my right and left sides as if they could siphon the truth from me. What were the lights for? A low hum buzzed, and I glanced upward. A cap descended from the tube's ceiling. Goose bumps pebbled my arms when the cap hovered within centimeters of my hair. Could it read my mind?

"Chill." Jethro's voice boomed through speakers. "What you're seeing is the latest in our illustrious government's polygraph technology. This ain't your grandma's poly, so get used to it if you wanna work as an agent."

"Let's get this over with."

"Not so fast. You gotta know how it works. The red beam's monitoring your heart rate and blood pressure. The blue your respiration."

"And the thing on my head?"

"I was getting to that." He scowled. "The cap monitors your body for minute physical changes related to body temperature. You so much as perspire one drop, that thing'll pick it up." He launched his wad of gum at the trash incinerator. "Sometimes people tell white lies, like if your friend gets a nasty haircut and you tell her it's cute. Your body always has a physiological response any time you lie. But. This machine don't know the difference between white lies and the big ones. So ya better tell the truth."

Fabulous.

"This test'll be a baseline to tell me how much deception training you need." He typed something and then looked up. "We gotta make sure the machine's working right. Look at the display in front of you." The monitor lit. "Pick a number, and write it with your left hand."

I wrote a seven.

From his seat, he scrawled the numbers five, six, eight, and nine on the screen to the left and right of my seven. "When I ask you if you wrote one of the numbers, you gotta answer no. When I get to seven, look at the number, think about writing it, and answer no."

He asked the questions, and I answered no to all of them. This was weird.

Jethro looked up. "I've got the instrument adjusted. Now, I'm gonna start with a few questions. Answer like you're trying to pass this poly in order to infiltrate the government. Ready?"

"Yeah." My stomach quavered, and a few seconds later, his mouth flattened.

"Today Monday?"

"Yes."

"Ever lied to your parents?"

"Yes."

"Ever stolen money?"

"No."

"Ever cheated on a test?"

I hesitated. Why did that matter? "No."

Jethro stood and walked from the room. What was he thinking? Was I doing okay? I tapped my foot against the orange footprint. I had to pass so I could help Ben. A few minutes later, Jethro returned. "Let's go on."

"Are the lights on in here?"

I frowned. What did that have to do with anything? "Yes."

"You planning to answer each question truthfully?"

"Yes."

"You the kind of person who'd betray a family member?"

I pictured my mother. "No."

"Ever committed an act of espionage against the United Regions of North America?"

Now these were the questions I'd expected. "No." Did hacking into government databases count?

"Is it August?"

"Yes." Weird.

"You ever been associated with anyone in the rebel movement?"

"No." I swallowed.

"You promise to swear allegiance to the United Regions of North America and her leader, President Cleatus Fortune?"

Fortune was a reptile. "Yes."

The red and blue light beams disappeared, tube's door slid open, and the cap ascended. "That's it for tonight," Jethro said.

"Did I pass?" I slipped from my glass prison and peered over his shoulder.

Jethro's mouth tightened into a thin line. "If you become a liberation agent, you might have to go undercover and apply for a government job. They'll grill ya like that for hours." He pointed to the data on the monitor. "You're one of the worst liars I've ever met."

Chapter 2

I lay motionless, not wanting to disturb the other girls in the bunkroom. Taking my courier from the shelf next to the top bunk, I checked the time—12:27. It'd been two hours since my encounter with Jethro, during which I'd replayed the scene in my mind a thousand times and questioned my decision to join the Emancipation Warriors.

But what else would I have done? Going back to my mother wasn't an option.

When I'd become pregnant and decided to run away to protect my baby from my country's pregnancy termination law for underage girls, I'd ruined my relationship with my mother. Breaking the law when your mother is a governor and presidential nominee will do that. Although her political career didn't have to be over if she kept her knowledge of my running away a secret. And if she could stop the corrupt President Fortune from hanging onto the presidency that should've been hers.

Would the evidence I'd given my mother be enough to convict Fortune of planning President Hernandez's assassination and attempting to take her out as well? I hoped so.

Then there was Ben Lagarde, who was captured, sitting in prison, and a large part of my motivation for joining the Emancipation Warriors.

I had to help him.

A siren's blast pierced my thoughts, and my hands flew to my ears. The lights in the room blinked to life, and the bed shook as the girl beneath me jumped out. Women of varying ages leaped from bunk beds and dressed quickly.

My bunkmate reached up and hit me on the arm. "Hey, New Girl. Don't just sit there. Get dressed. This is a drill. At least, I hope so."

I stared at the petite redhead for a few seconds before I climbed down and picked up the clothes that I'd tossed on my bag earlier. "What for?"

"We have to be prepared in case the government locates us." She pulled a sweatshirt over her short curls. They pulled taut before they sprang back into place. "I'm Agatha."

"Vivica." I was still trying to absorb this rapid change in pace. The other women in the room began to file out. I zipped my jeans. "Where am I supposed to go? I got here a few hours ago." I slipped on my shoes and fumbled with the laces.

Agatha put her hands on her hips and tapped her foot.

"Sorry." I straightened. "I'm ready."

She looked me up and down. "Follow me." She pushed through the swinging door into the hallway where an orange light pulsed in time with the siren. "As you know, the Warriors train agents here. Upstairs is a computer warehouse."

I chuckled. "Nice."

Agatha eyed me. "That way the government doesn't suspect what's really going on. Every so often, we practice taking our posts in the middle of the night. In case someone from the government shows."

Charging down the hall, she led the way up a narrow metal staircase, her footsteps clanging against the grating. The siren's continuous wail jabbed my sanity and scattered my thoughts. Why couldn't they shut it down?

We went through a door, and it shut behind us, sealing off the siren's yowls. We entered a large room with rows of metal shelves. Agatha grabbed a tablet and moved toward a stack of boxes. "If anyone asks, I'm training you to do inventory."

"Right."

All over the warehouse, workers took their places. An office lit up, and a woman wearing a long denim skirt darted inside and sat down at a desk. Two men whizzed by in a golf cart. I had more questions, but I bit my tongue when I realized that if someone overheard me asking, it might be disastrous. I kept my mouth shut and watched Agatha scan the boxes' barcodes with the tablet.

"Take a look." She showed me the program used for inventory and pointed at a row of boxes. "Go ahead. Scan them." She moved aside and allowed me to stand in her place. I obeyed. After my years of hacking databases and security systems, this was nothing.

"Now. Let me show you..." Her eyes fixated on something across the room.

Two men roamed and made notes on their couriers. They moved closer. One of the men was younger, and he wore a baseball cap. He paused next to us.

Agatha's voice quivered. "It's important these records are accurate so we don't mess up customers' orders."

Her hand shook slightly. Maybe it wasn't a drill. When the man passed, she sighed. I studied her, but her eyes gave me a warning to be quiet and keep scanning.

A shrill whistle blew a few minutes later. Agatha's shoulders slumped, and the sound of friendly chatter increased.

The man in the baseball cap returned to our post and held out his hand to Agatha. "Congratulations. You passed." He removed his cap and smoothed his wavy brown hair.

Agatha beamed and grasped his hand. "Thanks."

"Don't thank me. You dealt with the complication and followed protocol." He winked.

Agatha glanced at me. "She was cooperative."

I rolled my eyes. Not only was I a complication, but apparently, I was invisible. "Do either of you mind telling me what's going on? Besides flirting, of course."

Agatha glared.

He laughed, showing his dimples. "I'm Chad—a.k.a. Sleuthhound. I'm in charge of supervising drills and assessing agents in training. Agatha just passed a level in the field readiness test."

"I see." I smiled. "Congratulations."

Agatha's frown softened. "I have one more test to pass before they send me out."

"How long does this process take?"

"Three to six months, depending on the agent's skill level," Chad said. "Agatha is quite talented, so it's taken her three months."

I thought of Ben. I did *not* have three months to waste doing stupid training camp drills. I needed to be in the field as soon as possible. "What's the fastest an agent has ever completed training?"

Chad tapped his chin. "One guy completed training in a month. Rare though."

I vowed to complete the training in less than a month. "Who was it?"

"Drake Freeman."

That figured.

* * *

After the drill, we all filed downstairs to the bunkrooms, but an adrenaline rush like I'd just experienced wasn't conducive to sleep.

I pondered what Chad had told me about Drake, and my respect for him increased. Drake and I had our differences, but his skills and devotion to the Emancipation Warriors were worth emulating.

Then, I thought of Ben. How long would the government keep him in prison? What were the conditions like?

God, protect him. Keep him safe. Help me figure out a way to get him out, so we can be together.

A few more minutes passed while I beat my pillow into submission and tried to find a comfortable position on the thin mattress. Eventually the stirring and whispers from the other girls died away. Since sleep was impossible, I left the bunkroom. It was time to get a head start on figuring this place out. My own personal orientation.

I continued down the hallway until I came to a door labeled GYM. I pushed open the door, peered in, and saw what I expected—a room of treadmills, stationary bikes, and weight machines. Convenient but not interesting. As I continued on, the corridor came to a T, so I went left. At the end of the hall, a sliver of light illuminated the area.

I stopped when I heard Drake's voice. Hadn't he left earlier after dropping me off? Tiptoeing closer, I strained to listen.

"Jethro, you have to tell her," Drake said.

"Why's that?" Jethro sounded annoyed.

"Just trust me."

I moved closer. Were they talking about me? It was egotistical to assume so, but I had a feeling.

"I ain't so sure I do. You bring Genevieve Wilkins's kid here and expect me to roll out a welcome mat?"

Fear of what they were hiding spoiled the affirmation that my gut feeling was right. Was something wrong with my baby? Had I made a mistake giving him up for adoption?

"She's proven she's not like her mother. You have no idea what Vivica went through to save her child. The kind of situations she was able to get herself out of. She did things agents with years of experience couldn't have done. I'm telling you, she's one of the best assets this organization has, and your attitude is going to be a detriment if you don't watch it."

I sagged against the wall. I had no idea Drake thought these things about me.

"You think you're better than the rest of us 'cause you blew in and outta here in a month? Well, I call the shots at this camp, no matter how big you are in this organization, Cavalier."

I grinned. Drake's code name suited him perfectly. What would mine be?

"This isn't about your problem with me," Drake said. "It's about what's best for the Warriors."

"And your ego," Jethro said with a growl.

It was pretty apparent this was about *Jethro's* ego.

"It's been a long night," Jethro said. "I'm hitting the sack. Have a safe trip."

I scampered toward the end of the hall where I could duck around the corner before Drake caught me.

Behind me, the door slammed.

"Really, my dear? Eavesdropping? I wish I were surprised."

I whirled to face Drake, who was smirking. "What doesn't Jethro want to tell me?"

Drake's face grew serious, and he glanced over his shoulder before opening the closest door. He turned on the lights and motioned for me to join him in the paneled office. The dusty desk and moldy odor indicated it had been vacant for a while. He shut the door and pointed at the desk chair. "Have a seat."

I dropped into a desk chair and sent up a cloud of dust that made my eyes itch.

Drake leaned against the desk. "How much did you hear?"

"Why does that matter?" Had I missed something even more important? I rubbed my eyes.

"I want to know." A note of irritation crept into his tone.

I told him what I'd heard. "What did Jethro not want to tell me? Is my baby okay? Or maybe it's Ben." I wrapped my arms around my torso and expected to see mockery in Drake's expression, like I always did when we discussed Ben, but Drake's face was stoic. That could only be a bad sign.

He ran his fingers through his spiky blond hair. "It's not your son. Or Ben."

Air whooshed from my lungs. "Then what?"

Drake pulled his courier from his jacket pocket. "A few hours ago, after I dropped you off, one of my contacts passed along news that's going to break in about two hours, when the morning newscasts start." He hesitated. "I didn't want you to hear it on TV."

I closed my eyes. "It's my mother, isn't it?"

"Someone leaked the information that she had a chance to arrest you but let you go."

My throat tightened.

"A few hours ago, President Fortune had your mother taken into custody for participating in anti-government activity."

CHAPTER 3

My mind whirred. Who would've betrayed my mother? Her assistant Melvin Powers had seen me at her house the day before. But he was loyal. Wasn't he?

Could Martina Ward, my former bodyguard and President Fortune's confidant, somehow have discovered my visit? She already knew I'd found the incriminating evidence that tied President Fortune to the attempt on my mother's life. Perhaps, in order to protect the president and herself, she'd used this to discredit my mother.

I took a deep breath to steady my racing heart. "What about the evidence I gave her? Did the police take it?"

"I'm not sure. I only know what my contact told me."

I massaged my temples. "Okay. What's the plan? I need to get out of here and do something. I don't have time to waste on training."

"I was afraid you'd say that. That's probably why Jethro didn't want me to tell you. But I needed to be honest with you."

I was learning a lot about Drake tonight. Or at least what he thought about me. There was too much I didn't know about him.

He stood. "As much as I hate to admit Jethro's right, you need more training."

"But that's not what you told—"

He held up a hand. "When you were working for us before, you did freelance work under my supervision. Now that you've joined our group, you have to do things our way. It won't sit well with leadership if I pull you out of training camp early."

"So you're going to give in to Jethro?" This was the last bit of ammunition I had.

"Nice try, my dear." Drake laughed. "No. I'll let Jethro win."

"Why? It's obvious you can't stand the guy, and I heard what you said about my skills."

"Something I never would've said if I'd known you were listening. You're talented, but putting you in the field before you're ready and sending you on a mission to liberate people you care about is a bad idea."

"But I'd do a better job because of it. Don't you see? Ben needs me. Now my mother does too."

Drake scowled. "I thought joining the Warriors wasn't about Ben."

Why had I said that? "It's not just about Ben." I bit my lip. "It's about giving my son a chance at a normal life. Besides, Emma and Jesse need me too." Because of me, the four-year-old twins, whose parents had hidden me on their farm while I was pregnant, had lost their mother, and the Warriors suspected the government had transferred the kids to a reeducation center.

"Their father's looking for them."

"So, you're leaving me here to rot with Jethro the Jerk?" I was whining, but I didn't care.

"I may not get along with Jethro, but he's fair. Besides, I can't blame him for wanting to make sure you're loyal. If the government managed to get a mole in here, the consequences would be horrendous. But if I back off, maybe he'll come around. If you prove yourself."

"You mean *when* I prove myself." I stood and faced Drake.

He smiled. "Get back to bed before someone catches you."

I wanted to give a sharp retort, but Drake was right. I raised my chin. "Fine." I stalked around the desk to the door, but when I glanced over my shoulder at the handsome man who'd come to my rescue more times than I cared to admit, something inside me softened. "Be careful, Cavalier."

"Always." Drake's blue eyes twinkled. "Thanks for caring."

* * *

Ophelia Knox had created my first alias, Sarah Miller. According to the schedule on my courier, I was to report to Ophelia at 0700 so she could invent Fredrica Lloyd—code name, Storyteller. I gritted my teeth.

When I entered the workroom, Ophelia greeted me with a hug. Though she had the same short, black hair, she no longer wore cat-eye glasses.

She rested her hands on my shoulders and studied me. "Nice to see you. Still enjoying being a brunette?"

"No. I miss being blonde."

Ophelia smiled and played with one of her hoop earrings. "Then I have good news. I'm going to change your mousy brown hair back to blonde. I have some other tricks up my sleeve for turning you into Fredrica too." She pointed at the chair. "That name suits you, you know."

I sat. "How so?"

"More elegant. Sophisticated. Like your real name." Ophelia fastened a cape around my shoulders.

"Thanks. I like it too. My code name? Total insult."

She frowned. "Why?"

I told her about my polygraph test and how Jethro had said I was the worst liar he'd ever met.

She chuckled softly. "I'm sorry. Jethro does pick the code names. His is Heavyweight."

I snorted.

"Mine's Girl Friday. I don't love it, but it could be worse." Ophelia shook her head. "Don't you worry about that poly. A lot of people have trouble with that. This new look'll help. You know, make you feel more like Fredrica."

I glanced at the TV mounted on the wall. "Do you mind if we turn that on? I'd like to watch the news."

"No problem." She picked up her courier and used it as a remote. She chose the only news station available—the one the government controlled. A commercial blared.

I'd tossed and turned after talking to Drake, but I'd dozed right before the alarm had shrieked through the speakers at 0600. I'd reached for my courier, accessed the Emancipation Warrior News, and skimmed the brief paragraph about my mother's arrest.

It hadn't been enough. I needed details.

Ophelia stood in front of me with what appeared to be a motorcycle helmet. She tossed me a headband. "Put that on to keep the hair back from your face."

I did and frowned.

"This helmet's got a camera and computer on the inside that's going to take your facial measurements. I'll use those to create a mask that'll change your appearance and help you bypass facial recognition."

I peeked at the TV. Still a commercial.

"Keep your eyes open or close 'em. It doesn't matter. Some people like to keep 'em closed so they don't freak out when I seal the eye shield." She slipped the helmet onto my head. "Count to ten, and it'll be over." The shield and darkness enfolded my face, but green and orange lights blinked.

I shut my eyes and focused on the drivel coming from the TV. "This is Jacinda Jackson reporting live from the Great Lakes Region. Shortly after midnight, Great Lakes governor and former presidential nominee Genevieve Wilkins was arrested in her home on charges of aiding and abetting a fugitive and participating in anti-government activity."

Ophelia pulled the helmet from my head. The TV displayed footage of police leading my mother from the governor's mansion in handcuffs. My fingernails burrowed into my palm.

"It has come to our attention that Wilkins's underage daughter Vivica recently gave birth to a child. Our sources confirm that Vivica sought help from the rebels in order to break the term law, caused the death of Population Management Agent Axel Smythe, and injured two other people. Vivica is considered a fugitive, and anyone with information leading to her arrest will be rewarded."

I gasped. Had Drake left the details about me out purposely, or had he not known?

Ophelia rested a hand on my shoulder. "It's all gonna be okay, you know."

"The disguise will help."

"I wasn't talking about that. I meant God will take care of everything."

My throat was too swollen to speak, so I nodded as she went to work on my hair.

* * *

That evening, I rested on my bunk and projected pictures of my son Isaac from my courier on the wall opposite my bed. My head knew he was no longer mine since the adoption, but my heart hadn't gotten the message.

His adoptive mother had agreed to send pictures occasionally, but she hadn't yet. Of course, it had only been a few days since I'd left them.

"Whose baby?" Agatha leaned against the bunk and pointed at the wall.

"Mine." I told her my story.

"Wow. I had no idea." She fidgeted with a curl. "Are you okay? I mean, if you need to talk about it..."

I shrugged. "There's nothing to talk about. It's something I just have to deal with."

She nodded. "Look," she paused and pulled a Bible out from under her bunk and held it up. "I don't know how you feel about exclusivist Christians—"

"Don't call us that. I hate that term. Well, now I do." I grinned. "I didn't used to." Exclusivist was a term the media had given to Christians who believed Jesus Christ was the only way to heaven, unlike the United Evangelical Pluralists, who believed in many ways to heaven and had created the Revised Freedom Version of the Bible that was less offensive than the unedited, illegal versions.

"Cool. I mean, not all the Warriors are Christians, so I just wanted to check." She pointed to the Bible. "This is the real version. Some of the other girls and I are having a Bible study right now, if you'd like to come."

I shoved my courier in my pocket and leaped off the bed. "Definitely." It was time I figured out how to be a Christian.

* * *

The next morning, Jethro hunted me down and corralled me into a room full of cubicles where people worked at computers. He pointed toward an empty stall that contained a desk, a chair, and computer.

"Been thinking 'bout your polygraph disaster. Working behind the scenes is gonna be better for you, now that you're a fugitive. This room here is full of the best hackers in our organization, and they help our agents move around without our wonderful government knowing. They took care of you while you were hiding out. I met with 'em this morning, and they're actually impressed with your work."

My breath caught. Being stuck behind a computer during my pregnancy had been bad enough. Now they wanted to make it permanent? How would I help Ben? And what about Emma and Jesse? And now my mother?

"So you're going to stick me in here and forget about me? You didn't even try to train me to beat that polygraph. You saw my results and gave up."

Jethro's face reddened. "When you joined the Warriors, you gave up the right to call the shots. If I think the best place for you is behind a computer, then that's where you're gonna be. Got it?"

"No. You aren't even giving me a chance. Besides, I'll have a disguise if I work in the field."

"Let me spell it out for you. You're too twitchy. No one with your baseline has become a liberation agent. It ain't possible."

My stomach knotted. I refused to believe I was that bad at lying. I'd hidden my pregnancy for months. "Give me one more chance. I need a few days, and I'll be ready. I can do this. Wouldn't you rather give me one more shot than never know what might've been? If I don't pass, I promise I'll be a hacker—if you give me a new code name."

Jethro huffed. "I don't got time to waste training you. We're swamped right now."

"Can someone else?"

He ruminated on his gum. "Moonbeam's—Agatha's—deception scores are top notch, and she's already helping with your orientation."

"Please. Let her help me."

"You got one week."

Chapter 4

"Drake always said I was a terrible actress, but I thought I was a decent liar." I attacked my wet hair with a towel later that night while Agatha sat on the bottom bunk in our dorm.

She studied me. "I doubt it's as bad as Jethro led you to believe, or he'd never consider letting me help you. He may be trying to mess with your head."

"Did he do that to you?"

"He does that to everybody. Thinks it makes us tougher." She wound a red curl around her index finger. "I had to lie to survive before I got here, so deception was one of the easier things for me."

I shot her a dirty look, and she laughed.

"We won't talk about how long it took me to pass my physical exam. I'm a slow runner. We all have a weakness."

"I can't have a weakness." I told her about Ben and how he was in prison for helping me track down information about President Fortune. I took a deep breath. "I love him. Before I met Ben, I was too tough to fall in love. It was safer." I studied my hands. "It's probably stupid, but I have this dream of a normal life. That somehow everything will work out, and we'll be together when the war is over."

"It's not stupid. And I get it." Agatha smiled and leaned forward. "Chad means everything to me. I never thought I'd meet anyone like him. I can't imagine how I'd feel if he were in prison."

She didn't add the words, "because of me," but she was probably thinking them.

I snatched a comb and dragged it through my hair. "So you're a good liar. What's your secret?"

"There are two." She chewed her lower lip. "The polygraph is a game. Once you know the rules the examiner is using, it's easier to beat him. I have a few tricks I can share." She rummaged through her bag at the foot of the bed. "Did Jethro tell you what the cap over your head was for?"

"To monitor my physical responses."

She grinned. "So you believed him." She withdrew a ball of gray yarn with some sort of project attached to it.

My eyes widened. "You mean, it doesn't?"

"Nope." She started knitting. "It's there to psych you out. What was your gut reaction when you saw it come down out of the top of the machine?"

"That it was going to read my mind."

"Exactly. That's what you're supposed to think. That's the game."

I examined her project. "What're you making?"

"A hat. For Chad. What do you think of the color?"

Was gray even considered a color? "It's good for a guy."

"So diplomatic." She chuckled. "I see why you struggle with deception. Anyway, most of what our government does is a big game. You just have to figure out when they're bluffing."

Games I could handle. "What's the second secret?"

"You have to become your alias. What's her name?"

"Fredrica Lloyd."

"Cool. So Fredrica can't be a character you've read about on paper. Draw on your own experiences and emotions to make her real."

"You mean Fredrica needs a history?" It was so obvious. Why hadn't I thought of it sooner?

"Right. But that's only the beginning. You need to know why Fredrica wants to work for the government. What drives her? What are her passions? Her quirks. Habits. Hobbies. Ex-boyfriends. Favorite color. Is she a morning person or a night person?" Agatha paused and surveyed her progress on the hat. "You should know her so well that when you become her, you can't find yourself until you need to. Once you've done that, you'll be on your way."

* * *

I returned to Ophelia's workroom three days later, and she clasped her hands when she saw me. "I can't wait to see how this disguise turns out."

I hoped my new face looked as good as my hair that she'd restored to its natural color. Ophelia fastened the cape around my shoulders, and a new ring sparkled on her finger. I grabbed her hand.

"Engagement ring?" No wonder she was in such a giddy mood.

She squealed. "Yes!"

"Congratulations. So who's the guy?"

"Liam Freeman. He flew in for a meeting last night with Jethro and surprised me afterward."

I smiled. Liam was Drake's older brother. "When's the wedding?"

Ophelia laughed. "As soon as possible. We're not having a big shindig. It doesn't seem right with the war, you know?"

"He seems like a great guy."

"He is. So's his brother. I can't figure out how he got so hung up on that Faith chick." Ophelia shook her head and picked up the mask that would reshape my face. "The end of their relationship hit Drake hard."

"I couldn't tell. He's pretty good at hiding how he feels." That statement wasn't entirely truthful, because there was at least one time when Drake had seemed bothered, but I wanted to know what Ophelia would say.

She spread some adhesive on the mask. "No. You'd have to know Drake pretty well to see he was devastated. Took the wind out of his sails. He's been pretty bitter and cranky lately."

He hadn't been with me.

"Hold still." She bent down so she could see my face. "Drake likes to come across as a tough guy, but he has a kind heart. I've never been able to figure out why he likes to keep it hidden."

"Maybe he's afraid of getting hurt."

"Yeah. I'm afraid this thing with Faith has scarred him for life."

"He's tougher than that." I grimaced at my reflection, and Ophelia turned my chair away from the mirror.

"You're right. And he's been taking his walk with Jesus a little more seriously lately." She adjusted the mask and held it in place. "You doing okay with the fact your man's in prison?"

My heart skidded. "Ben's not officially my man, but I keep praying he'll be okay." And that we'd be together again someday.

She grabbed some foundation. "That's the best thing we can do right now." She dabbed the makeup on my face. "It's probably the only thing we can do."

She turned me back toward the mirror. "Here you go. Vivica, meet Fredrica Lloyd."

I gripped the arms of the chair. Fredrica's nose was fuller than mine, and her chin was sharper. Fredrica's face was regal, though it wasn't beautiful. The entire mask appeared like real skin. The mouth piece fit over my teeth and changed the shape of my mouth and teeth. It had a chip that altered my voice as I spoke. I studied my reflection and thought about Fredrica's story. Did she like her appearance? No.

She wanted to be prettier so more boys would like her.

"What do you think?"

"You do your job well."

"Thanks. God's handiwork is prettier than my own, but your real beauty could get you arrested." She fluffed my bangs. "Jethro and Liam will be pleased."

"Great."

"I'm finished here, and I need to get going." She handed me a bag. "This has an extra mask, makeup, and directions on how to apply it. If you even need it. The masks are reusable, and you can leave 'em on for weeks at a time because the material is breathable and waterproof." She gave me a quick hug. "God bless."

* * *

That afternoon when I left my training at the firing range, a message blinked on my courier.

`Attention all agents and trainees: Report to the briefing room for a mandatory meeting at 1800.`

When I found the briefing room, there was standing room only in the back. I wanted to lean against the wall, but since everyone else stood at attention, I did the same. At precisely 1800, Jethro went to the front.

"We coulda sent this information out on your couriers, but it's too important for anyone to miss. I'll let the video speak for itself." He stepped aside, and President Fortune appeared on the screen. The time stamp in the lower right corner indicated he'd given this speech several hours earlier.

"Citizens of the United Regions of North America, it is with great sadness that I address you today. First, I'd like to comment on the unfortunate arrest of the former presidential nominee, Governor Genevieve Wilkins. When information came to light indicating that the governor had broken the law, I fulfilled my duty to uphold the laws of this land. I have no further comment on this situation."

Of course he didn't.

The president continued. "As you're aware, we're at war, and that is the main reason I'm speaking to you."

He paused as if he needed to let that non-revelation sink in.

"In times of war, leaders find themselves in difficult positions. It is from such a place that I address you. With the recent increase in rebel and anti-government activity inflamed by exclusivist Christian principles, I've found it necessary to issue an executive order. Beginning tomorrow, we will start executing those who have been imprisoned for anti-government activities or for violating the Peace and Unity Act by distributing unauthorized versions of the Bible and spreading exclusivist principles."

A collective gasp intruded upon the president's speech. I sagged against the wall.

"I hope by instituting such a policy, we are able to turn the tide against this so-called revolution and discourage citizens from becoming involved. I believe my predecessor and the governors of our great nation have been well-intentioned, but they have not been tough enough on those who express harmful and divisive beliefs. My action is necessary in order to preserve the peace and unity in our nation."

Yeah. Right.

"Understand that in order for someone to be executed, there must be irrefutable evidence of the person's guilt."

How much evidence did they have against my mother? Or Ben?

"Thank you for your cooperation in this matter, and I assure you that I take the safety of our nation very seriously. Good afternoon."

The screen faded to black.

CHAPTER 5

Tears blurred my vision, and the room's anguished silence thickened as those with imprisoned loved ones turned to friends for comfort.

I had no one.

I clenched my teeth and refused to cry as I fled the room. Not when I had to prove myself. Blinking the moisture from my eyes, I forced my mind away from Ben and my mother and on to Fredrica's story.

But I couldn't concentrate.

I pushed into the restroom and enclosed myself in a stall. Too many events had rocked my world in such a short amount of time. News of my mother's execution wasn't a surprise, but my helpless feeling was. As much as I worried about the injustice surrounding her upcoming death, I was more concerned that she might spend eternity in hell because she'd never accepted Jesus Christ as her Savior.

I'd only recently learned the truth. Why hadn't I shared it with her when I'd had the chance?

Because I'd been too worried about Ben.

And myself.

"God," I whispered, "please give me one chance to tell my mother about you. I won't waste it. And Lord, please stop the executions." I squeezed my eyes shut. "Protect Ben."

A door squeaked. "Vivica?"

Agatha. I took a deep breath, flushed the toilet, and exited the stall.

She threw her arms around me. "I saw you fly out of the meeting." She let go, and her eyes searched mine. "I'm so sorry about your mom. And Ben. I'm going to do everything I can to help you pass that poly. I've got some free time tomorrow afternoon." She squared her shoulders. "You're going to pass, and you'll help save the people you love. Got it?"

The lump in my throat was so large, I only managed to nod.

* * *

The next afternoon, I practiced at the firing range. After several sessions with the Diablo 87, my aim had improved, and I was more comfortable handling a gun. Even though my former bodyguard Bobby had taught me how to use this type of weapon several years ago, I'd never had a chance to practice regularly because the United Regions of North America had banned firearms for citizens except antique hunting rifles that could only be used on designated hunting preserves. Bobby had been allowed to carry a gun because he'd been a government employee.

Agatha burst into the room. I secured my weapon and faced her.

"Carry on." She motioned toward my target. "I'll ask you questions while you're practicing."

"But—"

She pointed to my target. "The shots aren't exactly clustered together. You could use more practice."

"Thanks."

"No problem." Agatha grinned. "So, Fredrica, why do want to work for the government?"

I turned back toward my target, picked up the gun, and focused on Fredrica's story. "I want to help keep citizens safe, especially children." I aimed and fired.

"That's noble, but that's something every person who applies says. How are you different?"

I gave a half smile. "Ten years ago, my little sister Hannah died in a domestic terrorist attack. She was playing at the park when a bomb detonated nearby." I turned my thoughts to the people who'd given their lives protect me. Tears welled in my eyes. "She was killed instantly. It's a terrible day when all you have to be grateful for is that your nine-year-old sister didn't suffer when she died." I fired again. "The rebels murdered my sister. I want them to pay." I hoped the story worked because for years, the media had blamed every act of evil in our nation on the rebels, even though the Emancipation Warriors had never been involved. Until now.

"Awesome story." She gave a thumbs-up and then slipped back into her interviewer role. "Do you have a boyfriend?"

"Boys ignore me. I'm not pretty enough. Or popular."

"What's your favorite store?"

"I hate to shop."

Agatha raised an eyebrow. "Then you'll need to look frumpy. Favorite food?"

I hesitated. "Peanut butter."

"You can't hesitate. And, seriously. *Peanut butter* is your fav?"

"Don't judge. Besides, if you asked the real me, I'd waver because I like several things equally."

"Then say that." Agatha chewed her lip. "Let's talk about the poly, because that's harder."

"Good."

"Did Jethro do a stim test?"

"What's that?"

"Did he tell you to write a number and ask you to lie about it?"

"You mean that whole weird thing was a test? I thought he was adjusting the equipment." I removed the ammo from the Diablo, cleaned it, and put it away.

"Exactly. That's what he wanted you to think. Jethro's a good guy, but he has to play the role of a government examiner whose job is to convince you that he knows when you're lying. Even if your body didn't show a reaction when you lied about writing the number, it's his job to make you believe it did. That's the point of a stimulation test."

"You weren't kidding when you said the poly's a game."

"Right. Let me give you a few more tips on how to win."

* * *

Two days later, I stood inside the polygraph's glass tube and refused to allow myself to feel nervous when the beams spotlighted me and the cap floated above my head. Jethro pretended to appear busy as he sat behind the monitors. Knowing that making me wait was part of the game, I allowed my mind to drift to a happy and peaceful time, as Agatha had instructed.

I thought of Ben and the time we'd picnicked next to a creek one autumn Saturday almost a year ago. Orange, rust, and yellow leaves danced against an azure sky while the afternoon sun warmed us. Later, we paddled a canoe down the creek, dodging boulders.

When a bee landed on my arm, I almost overturned the canoe, but Ben held our vessel steady. I collapsed into his arms and laughed. Then I gazed into his eyes, and he kissed me.

Someday I'd feel his arms around me again.

Jethro cleared his throat. "We're ready."

He performed another stim test, but I followed his instructions and answered no to all of the questions.

"Are the lights on in this room?"

"Yes." I took slow even breaths.

"Ever committed an act of espionage against the United Regions of North America?"

Before I answered, I let my mind wander back to Ben's kiss. To the light that shined in his chocolate eyes. "No."

Jethro interrogated me for at least another hour before he opened the tube's door. "We're done."

"Did I pass?"

He sniffed. "I'll let you know."

Chapter 6

I let the shower's warm mist rinse my fears away while I recalled Jethro's guarded tone. Maybe I needed to accept I'd never work in the field. I turned off the water and wrapped myself in a towel. I'd removed my Fredrica mask because, even though the material was waterproof, it still made my skin itch.

I reached for my clothes, and the siren began to wail. Great timing for a drill. I sighed and began to dress quickly. The bathroom door swung open, and a fist pounded the partition that enclosed the shower.

"Hurry up," Agatha said. "I already lost time looking for you."

I finished dressing, and since there wasn't time to reapply my mask, I tucked it into my waistband beneath my shirt and followed her into the hall. Since this was only my second drill, I relied on her for direction. We climbed the stairs to the warehouse floor. She reached for the door handle at the top of the stairs as staccato pings of machine gun fire sounded and clashed with screams.

My stomach plummeted.

With her hand frozen on the door, she whipped around to face me. Her ghastly expression was magnified by the sputtering orange light. *Thump.* The door rattled. Her eyes widened, and she clattered down the stairs, came back up, grabbed my arm, and dragged me around the corner.

She fought to catch her breath. "Has to be the government."

My heart thudded. All of our fellow Warriors were upstairs on the warehouse floor. "How do we get out?" Panic threatened, but I refused to surrender to its grasp. Had someone figured out I was here?

Agatha hauled me back to the dorm, released my arm, and tossed the mattress off her bed. The dingy green blanket pooled on the floor. Opening a compartment beneath the bed, she slung a backpack over her shoulder and dumped another at my feet. I snatched my bag of makeup supplies and stuffed it in the backpack along with my mask.

Agatha removed a tranquilizer gun from a cabinet by the door. I put on the backpack, and she handed the tranq gun to me and put one in her ankle holster. Then she took a Diablo 87 from the cabinet. "Let's go."

We ran into the hallway, and there was another thud against the metal door at the top of the stairs. Blood flowed beneath the door's crack and dripped through the metal grating, forming a puddle on the concrete below.

I shuddered.

She led us down the hall past Jethro's darkened office.

Agatha pushed through an emergency door, and I followed. A blast behind us shook the ground so hard I stumbled into the dark tunnel. She pulled the door shut and punched in a code on the keypad next to it. "That'll buy us about thirty seconds."

She used her courier as a flashlight and started running. Behind us, someone pounded on the door. With each thud, we increased our speed. I struggled to keep pace since it had only been a few weeks since I'd given birth. Gulping air, I tried to ignore the fiery pains.

"How far do we have to go?" I asked.

"This tunnel leads to a substation a quarter mile from here. If they haven't found it, we'll be able to take a vehicle and get out of here," Agatha said as we continued running.

Finally, we stopped in front of a door. She wrenched it open and motioned for me to go ahead. An explosion shook the tunnel, and specks of dirt rained on our head. Shouts.

I led the way with my flashlight and climbed the stairs.

"Faster," Agatha said. "I couldn't lock it."

I had to stay focused or I could cause our deaths. The faces of those who'd died because of me in the past rose from the depths where I'd tried to bury them, and while I raced up the stairs, I blinked away their images.

But they haunted me.

When we reached the top of the stairs, Agatha brushed by me and drew her gun. Putting her ear against the door, she waited. Then she turned. "I don't hear anything," she whispered.

Please, God, don't let us walk into an ambush.

The door protested as she eased it open, and I cringed. She glimpsed quickly from side to side.

"It's clear." She entered.

The narrow room was like an empty closet. Another door blocked us. Agatha listened. Her eyes widened, and she put a finger to her lips and motioned for me to come closer.

My throat thickened. Had the government troops made it to the substation?

"How many dead?" an older man's voice asked.

"Twenty-seven rebels," a young voice said in a smug tone.

I covered my face and drew a ragged breath as I thought about the kind people I'd worked with during the past couple of weeks. I tried to calculate how many Warriors were at the training camp. Was there hope that some had eluded the troops? I dropped my hands and clenched my fists.

"There's no need to sound so proud of yourself," the older man said. "Twenty-seven rebels would've brought a hefty price. Now we've got nothing. You pull a stunt like that again, and I'll turn you in as one of them."

My brow wrinkled. What was he talking about?

"But they fought back," the young voice said. He had to be at least eighteen to work for the government, but this kid sounded more like he was twelve.

"Never mind, you two," a woman's voice growled. "Is that Wilkins girl here?"

Chapter 7

My hand flew to my mouth to push in the sound that fought to be set free. A whimper escaped. Agatha silenced me with a fierce stare.

"No," the older man said. "But some rebels escaped."

My breath came in choked gasps.

"Not. Acceptable," the woman said. "We need Wilkins in custody. I don't wanna report back to Officer Ward that we didn't find her. Besides, I want my cut of the reward money."

"Ma'am, there're rebel training camps everywhere. She could be at any one of them. We'll get her."

Twenty-seven people dead. Because of me.

Something buzzed. It was probably an MD3, the device the government issued to all its employees.

"Excellent," the woman said. "That was Officer Taylor. There's a tunnel that leads away from the warehouse to this substation. Rebels are headed here now."

"So where's the exit?" the teenager asked.

"Do I look like I have a map in my head? Start searching, moron," the woman said. "Officer Fuentes, come with me. We need to figure out how many escaped and find them."

Two sets of footsteps sounded against the floor and grew fainter.

I turned to look at Agatha. The desperation on her face had to reflect my own terror. I studied the ceiling, hoping to see air ducts or something we could crawl through. Nothing.

Then a single set of footsteps sounded in the room. We lined the wall where the door would open and give us cover. I was on the outside, but Agatha traded places with me and holstered her weapon. "I'll surprise him," she whispered, "and you hit him with a tranq dart."

My head bobbed as I drew the gun. My hands shook, and I took a deep breath to steady myself.

The door opened, and a thin figure stood silhouetted in the doorway. I caught a glimpse of the boyish face before Agatha blasted her fist into his throat and kicked him in the crotch. He fell to his knees, and I shot the tranq gun. The dart pricked his upper arm. Agatha got him in a headlock, clapped her hand over his mouth, and restrained him while he thrashed. When he collapsed, she took his machine gun, a Demonio 57.

The room where the officers had been standing was an office. We exited into a long corridor. Agatha motioned to the left, and I followed. When a soldier rounded the corner and fired at us, she aimed and shot back with the Demonio.

He dropped, and my hand flew to my mouth. I'd never thought the revolution was a game, but now it became too real as his vacant eyes stared toward heaven.

"Grab his gun," she said.

In a trance, I obeyed, and we continued down the passageway. She halted at a metal door and held the machine gun up. Slowly, she opened the door and stepped through.

I held my breath.

"Clear," Agatha said.

I followed her into the garage crammed with black service

vehicles. Wasn't this the first place the goons would look? Did they not know it was here? Agatha led us to an SUV parked closest to the door. She headed for the control seat and began programming the vehicle using the dashboard computer.

Something didn't feel right. "Wait," I said.

"What?" Agatha glared. "They're going to find us any second."

"Give me a minute to disable the tracking."

She glanced over her shoulder. "Why wouldn't we want the Warriors to know where we are?"

"If the government found this training camp, we can't assume any technology is safe. They could hack the system and find this SUV." Using my courier, I accessed the network, disconnected the vehicle from the Warrior's tracking program, and made sure it was invisible to the government's surveillance program. "We're good to go."

Agatha handed me the Demonio. "Hold this. I can't do two things at once."

She started the engine, and when the SUV backed itself out of the garage, two soldiers started firing on us.

The high-beam headlights blinked on, and the vehicle propelled itself forward. One of the soldiers jumped into the SUV's path, and the brakes stopped us inches in front of the man.

I jammed the manual override button the Warriors had installed on the dashboard when they'd customized the SUV. The soldier leveled his Demonio at us through the windshield. We ducked.

"Hit the accelerator!" I shouted.

"I am. It's not going!"

"Argh!" What a time for a slow computer.

The solider fired and the windshield shattered, spraying glass on our heads. Sliding to my knees and peeking above the dashboard, I shoved the machine gun out of the windshield and pulled the trigger as the car lurched forward. The man leapt from our path, and we sat up and sped down a tree-lined gravel drive. Bugs splattered onto our faces.

Behind us, an SUV hovered, and the headlights nearly disappeared. They had to be driving manually because the vehicle's system would never allow it to follow so closely.

"Faster, Agatha!" I shrieked.

"I'm pushing it as fast as it'll go!"

When I turned to the front, a buck jumped into our path. We screamed as Agatha swerved, sideswiping a tree. The rearview mirror flicked off, but she jerked the SUV back onto the road. I whipped around in time to see the buck skidding over our pursuers' windshield, leaving a trail of blood in its wake.

The driver lost control, veered across the road, and then crashed into trees on the opposite side. Within seconds the men hopped out and started shooting. Agatha put distance between us, and when we reached the main road, we spun tires out of their line of fire.

* * *

Thirty miles south of the Warehouse was a city with an Emancipation Warriors safe house, and after taking several detours down back roads and side streets to ensure we weren't followed, Agatha parked our battered SUV in a garage in the back of an unassuming two-story apartment building.

We hid our weapons in our bags and filed up the outdoor staircase, into apartment 234. I bolted the door behind us before collapsing on the threadbare couch ornamented with hibiscus. The apartment smelled of garlic and burnt toast as if someone had been there recently. Agatha raced down the hall and peeked into the open doors before returning to the living room.

"Chad's not here." Agatha swiped the back of her hand over her eyes. "I hoped…I prayed he'd make it out." She dropped her head into her hands and sobbed.

This was the first time I'd seen a crack in her tough armor. I rubbed her back. "He may show up. We'll pray that he does."

She drew a shuddering breath. "I know I'm supposed to trust God for everything, but sometimes it's so hard."

"Yeah. I have trouble understanding why he lets so many bad things happen."

"We all do."

We leaned back on the couch, stared at the wall, and sat in silence.

When my mind finally began to process all that had happened, I had a few questions. "How many agents were at the training facility?" I leaned forward.

She raised her head. "Around forty."

Twenty-seven dead. There was still hope Chad and others were alive. "Should we go back and look for survivors?"

"Absolutely not. Are you crazy?" Agatha said. "By the way, any ideas on how they knew to look for you at the Warehouse?"

I studied my hands. "No."

"Someone had to have leaked your location."

"That's not true. You heard them. They weren't certain I was there. This wasn't my fault."

"I never said it was." She crossed her arms and refused to meet my eyes.

I needed to change the subject. "What's next? How long do we stay here? Who do we contact?"

"I don't know. And I'm not sure I care."

I took my courier from my pocket and held it up. "I'm contacting Drake." I entered the codes I'd memorized to access Drake's secure line. When he didn't answer, I left a message letting him know what had happened and where we were.

Now, we had to wait.

* * *

Whap. Whap. Whap.

I sat up on the couch and clutched a pillow. It took a second for me to remember I was at the safe house. The bluish light of the television flickered in the darkened room, and a news anchor droned on about something the government-controlled media deemed important.

Whap. Whap. Whap.

I found the Diablo in my bag, headed for the door, and peered through the peephole. Chad. I swung open the door, and he stumbled in. The first hints of dawn edged the horizon as I locked the door behind him.

Tiny scratches marred his face, and his shirt was torn. A bloody bandage encircled his upper arm. He shuffled to the couch and sank down. "Water."

I scrambled to the kitchen as Agatha appeared, yawning and running her hands through her curls.

"What's going—?" She screeched and ran to Chad who held her tight. "You made it. I was so worried." She buried her head in his shoulder.

"I almost didn't. A few of us close to the door fought back, but when they outgunned us, we ran. This is a huge hit to the Emancipation Warriors." He squeezed the bridge of his nose. "I don't know how they found us…could be a mole…database breach…"

I wondered the same thing and didn't like thinking about the possibility there might be a mole. But it wouldn't be the first time that had happened. "Who else survived?"

"Jethro and several others. They're headed to another camp. He sent me here to locate anyone else who may have escaped."

My stomach lurched. "What about Ophelia?"

"She wasn't with Jethro, but she may have already left the Warehouse."

I prayed that was true and refocused on our situation. "Did you guys happen to disconnect your vehicles from the Warrior network?"

"No. Why?"

I groaned. "Call Jethro and tell him to disconnect in case the government's hacked our system." I said. "I'll go take care of your vehicle."

"Got it." He walked out of the room to make the call.

As I descended the stairs and entered the parking lot, the rising sun revealed chipped paint, crumbled sidewalks, and overgrown landscape. I found Chad's vehicle and severed it from the network.

My courier buzzed on my way back to the apartment. "Hey, Cavalier." I filled Drake in on Chad's arrival.

"Please tell me you're still in the safe house."

"Yes." I was *at* the safe house. Did one little preposition matter?

"Good. Because the government's increasing the number of cameras with facial recognition and retinal scanners. Even in rural areas. They believe it'll help track fugitives—"

"And now that I'm—" I froze. I never should've set foot outside of the safe house without wearing my Fredrica disguise, and even that was incomplete. A doctor hadn't changed my retinas. How many cameras had Agatha and I passed the night before?

"Storyteller? What's wrong?"

"Nothing." I kept my face down and flew upstairs.

"Don't lie to me."

I hesitated. "Last night. When Moonbeam and I fled, I wasn't in disguise. And no one's changed my eyes. They were going to do that today…" Why hadn't I taken the time to put on the mask?

I'd just turned the corner to get to the apartment, when headlights reflected against a window. I stopped, peered around the corner, and my knees weakened.

It was a government vehicle.

Chapter 8

"Cavalier, I've got to go."

Before he could protest, I hung up and burst into the apartment. "They found us."

Agatha and Chad vaulted off the couch and ran down the hall, and I scrambled to the bedroom to grab my bag.

We converged at the door, and I removed the baseball cap from Chad's head.

He frowned. "What are you—?"

I put it on, stuffing my hair underneath. "I'm a fugitive, remember? The cameras must've picked up my face or scanned my retinas last night."

Agatha thrust a pair of oversized sunglasses in my hand. "These *might* help. Keep your face down."

I slipped on the sunglasses as we ran for the staircase at the rear of the building.

We took the stairs as quietly as possible, and when we reached the corner, Chad stopped and held up a hand. He looked both ways before motioning us forward. There was a shout behind us followed by the sputter of gunfire. We sprinted to Chad's vehicle.

"Get in back and stay down, Storyteller." Chad leaped into the driver's seat and hit the manual override button. He revved the engine, and we shot forward.

More gunfire pinged.

The window buzzed, and Agatha returned fire.

Silence.

"What's happening?" I started to raise my head.

"Stay down," Chad said. "We're headed to the interstate." The car veered right.

"They got in their car. They'll catch up with us soon."

"Not with me driving."

I rested my cheek against the rough floor mats. Did he know the location of another training camp? My courier buzzed. Drake.

"They found us." I brought him up to speed.

"Put me on speaker. I need to talk to Sleuthhound."

I swiped my courier, and Drake's voice boomed through the car's speakers. I rolled on my back so I could see.

"Change of plans. Get to a safe place. Use your contacts to get disguises for Storyteller and Moonbeam. Do *not* bring them anywhere near the Zoo until you've changed their identities. We think the government used cameras to trace the path I took with Storyteller when I brought her to the Warehouse. It took them a while to zero in on the Warehouse's location."

My hand flew to my mouth. How many more people would die because of me? I forced myself to focus on Chad and Drake's conversation.

"Yes sir," Chad said. "What should I do with my own ID?"

"Let your superiors decide."

What was Drake talking about? Wasn't *he* Chad's superior?

"So you're permitting me to disclose information?" Chad asked as the car swerved right once again.

"Yes, but no more than necessary."

"Understood."

I sighed. What was with this cryptic conversation?

"Storyteller, listen to me," Drake said. "Do *not* use your new alias until we've had a chance to do your eye surgery. We've put a lot of work into that disguise, and I don't want you blowing it."

"Okay," I said.

"What's your status?" Drake asked.

Agatha glanced over her shoulder. "We've lost them."

Drake wished us well, and when we disconnected, the only sound was the hum of the tires against the road.

"Moonbeam, there's something I need to tell you," Chad said.

Uh oh. That didn't sound good.

"What?" Her voice was a hoarse whisper.

He accelerated. Surely he wasn't going to break up with her right now. Seconds ticked by. "Just tell us already!"

"About what Cavalier was saying…I'm not who you think I am."

"What do you mean?" she asked.

"I'm not a citizen of your country. I'm from the European Union and have been working cooperatively with your rebel organization for the last year and a half." A British accent replaced his North American one.

Agatha laughed. "You've got to be kidding."

"No. I'm quite serious."

"So everything you told me is a lie."

"Not everything. I love you. And I wanted to tell you…but couldn't until Cavalier permitted me."

"Tell me this. If we weren't in this situation where you had permission, would you ever have told me?" She crossed her arms.

He waited too long to answer.

"That's what I thought." She mumbled some things under her breath that I couldn't understand. It was probably just as well.

"I would've eventually," he said. "Surely you understand the need for secrecy."

"What's that supposed to mean?"

"You're not exactly honest with everyone you meet. You don't tell them *your* real name."

I stifled a gasp. What was her real name?

"That's different. You've always known, and I've never *lied* to you!" Agatha glanced over her shoulder at me. "I'm not telling. Safety reasons."

I pursed my lips. "Wasn't planning to ask."

But I did have another question Chad might be able to answer. "Why'd the Warriors let you in?"

"They want allies while they attempt to establish a new government, in order to keep the Council of World Peacekeepers from taking over the country."

"But why get involved?" I asked.

"We're very disturbed by the injustices in your government. We believe freedom is always in the best interest of every country because of the effect it has on the rest of the world. However, the identities of those of us from Europe have been concealed because Europe cannot give public support," he said. "Think monetary. Sharing of information."

"Because of the Council of World Peacekeepers?"

"Precisely," he said. "We're not thrilled by the power grab Council members have made. Many Europeans do not want a global government."

"I see."

Agatha bristled. "I can't believe you expect me to trust you after you've lied to me for an entire year."

"You need to trust me if you want to live. We're a bit desperate." His sharp tone made me cringe. He should try to be a little more understanding.

Chad used his courier to contact someone, and they used vague terminology to arrange a safe meeting place. An hour later, the vehicle slowed, and I sat up. A graffiti-covered sign stood next to a small church with paint peeling from the white siding and boarded windows. A line of pine trees served as a windbreak around the property. Chad parked in back next to a black sedan and got out. "Wait here."

Agatha climbed out, so I did the same. Chad shook his head.

A dark-skinned woman with a chin-length bob leaned against the sedan. She wore a sleeveless shirt that exhibited her toned arms.

"Can we trust them?" she asked in a clipped British accent.

"Yes. This is my girlfriend Moonbeam and her friend Storyteller," Chad said.

"Ex-girlfriend," Agatha said.

Chad's face fell.

She eyed Agatha and me. "Very well. My name is Tessa, and if I'm going to provide temporary identification and safe passage to your training camp, then I insist on certain conditions."

She was a spy. Of course there'd be conditions. "What?"

Tessa held out her courier and moved closer to me, angling it so I could see the picture of a man with a scraggly beard and vacant eyes.

Jared Canton.

He was the man who'd supplied me with incriminating evidence against President Fortune.

Tessa tilted her head. "You recognize him."

"What do you need?"

"Canton worked undercover for the Emancipation Warriors. It's our understanding he worked closely with Martina Ward, who's President Fortune's confidant."

"Yes, that's true." I wasn't giving away anything important by confirming that point.

"We believe he may have information about Ms. Ward and President Fortune's activities that have international repercussions, but unfortunately, Canton is well hidden. Our agents have been unable to find him, and the Emancipation Warriors have been unwilling to cooperate with us on this matter. If I provide safe passage, then I want your word that you'll use your skills to locate Canton so we can talk to him."

Canton wasn't exactly the chatty type, but I wasn't about to agree to give him up.

Not after he'd helped me.

"No deal. I'm not betraying him. If he's in hiding, and the Warriors won't cooperate, it's for a good reason." I glanced at Agatha who nodded slightly. "We'll figure something else out."

"Very well." Tessa turned back to her car. "I need to be on my way."

"Wait," Chad said. "What if we let Storyteller find Canton and talk to him herself? She can pass on information without revealing his location."

"I'll agree if she records the conversation," Tessa said.

"And I'll agree when I know what I'm asking Canton about."

Tessa lifted her chin. "The Peacemaker."

"What's that?" I frowned. "A weapon? Politician?"

"That's what we're trying to discover. We believe Martina is involved with the Peacemaker Project, and we want to know if Canton has intel about what it is."

"Fine. I'll attempt to find him and ask him what he knows."

"Because of the risk I'm taking in transporting you to the Zoo, I *expect* you to do so."

I held out my hand, and she grasped it.

* * *

Agatha and I waited in the back seat of our vehicle for Tessa and Chad to finish talking outside.

"You handled Tessa well." Agatha smiled. "I can't wait 'til Cavalier finds out about your little side mission. Especially since the Warriors didn't want to work with them on this."

"He'll have to be okay with it." There was always a chance Drake might not care.

"He has to do that a lot with you, doesn't he?"

How would she know that? "Are you saying I have a reputation?"

"Definitely. Before you came to the Warehouse, Heavyweight assigned you to me and briefed me on your background."

"Coming from him, that couldn't have been good."

"I take the negative things he has to say and cut them down by three-fourths."

"I appreciate that."

I looked out the window at Chad and Tessa. How much longer were they going to take? "Are you doing okay with…?" I pointed to Chad.

Her lips tightened into a thin line before she spoke. "Ask me again in six months."

Two sedans pulled into the parking lot, and Tessa opened the door. "Get out. We're taking my car to the airfield," she said. "The Zoo is in the Atlantic Region." She handed us each a small contact case and a bag. "The government believes we're European diplomats traveling with an entourage. Even though we're taking a charter flight, you'll have to fool the retinal scanners."

I examined the case. "I thought contacts didn't work. What about facial recognition?"

"They don't have cameras installed at this airfield yet. Another week and you'd be out of luck. The special contacts will be good enough because they have a chip that will project a false retina over your own. The screeners will believe you're part of our entourage and won't want to cause an international incident by asking members of a diplomat's team to remove contacts." She motioned toward the dilapidated church. "Go and change."

I walked toward the building and hoped Tessa was telling us the truth.

Chapter 9

When I finished dressing in the navy suit and put on the glasses Tessa had provided, I checked my reflection in the splotchy mirror inside the musty ladies' restroom. Though the church hadn't been used for years, the aroma of stale coffee lingered.

Agatha had changed into a cream-colored pantsuit and stood next to me while scowling at her likeness. "This suit washes me out."

Tessa laughed as she walked in. "Give me your couriers." We did, and a few minutes later, she returned them. "Check them for your temporary IDs."

Tessa had installed an electronic European passport and software so the courier mimicked the government issued multiphone devices, which were known as docs. I scrolled through the information. My name was Amelia Beaumont, and I was from the French region of Europe.

"What's your name?" I asked Agatha.

She glanced up from her courier. "Bridget O'Connor."

I snickered.

"What?"

"They had to give the redhead an Irish name, didn't they?"

Agatha's mouth quirked and her eyes danced. "Shut up."

We exited the church and took a circuitous route to the airfield to avoid cameras. When we reached the airfield, Chad drove onto the tarmac and parked next to the waiting jet. Two uniformed guards stood next to steps leading into the jet.

"I don't suppose I have to tell you to stay calm," Tessa said.

I looked at Agatha and rolled my eyes. At least this was good practice for my deception training.

"I'm not going with you," Chad said.

Agatha's fist clenched. "Why?"

"There's something else I have to take care of."

"What?"

"I can't tell you."

"Big surprise."

He turned to face her. "I really do love you."

"I know," Agatha said as we got out of the car. "But right now, that's not enough." She slammed the door and stalked toward the plane.

I clutched the car door. If Ben had kept this secret from me, would I have understood? Or would I have been as angry as Agatha? I wasn't sure, but his impending execution gave me a different perspective. Chad swallowed hard, and his eyes followed Agatha.

"I'm sorry," I said. "I'll talk to her."

He grasped my hand. "Thank you. Look after her, will you?"

"I'll do my best."

I followed Agatha and Tessa to the plane where a male guard stood armed with a Demonio 57. Tessa handed the female guard her courier. The woman, who had dark brows begging to be shaped, examined it and returned it. Then she held up a boxy device. "Look straight ahead."

Seconds passed, and finally a friendly beep sounded. "Go ahead," the woman said, and Tessa strode up the stairs and onto the plane.

Agatha was next. After the woman checked and returned her passport, she scanned Agatha's eyes. I held my breath, hoping that the contacts worked. A few seconds later, the scanner beeped, and Agatha moved forward.

I handed the woman my courier with a smile. I tried not to stare, but my eyes kept fixating on her uni-brow. She returned the courier with a scowl. "State your business."

That's what I got for gawking. For a second I considered pretending I didn't know English, but that would immediately make me suspicious. "I am an assistant to the diplomat," I said in a French accent. I prayed she wouldn't expect me to say anything in French. Though I was fluent in Spanish and Mandarin because of the nannies and tutors I'd had when I was younger, my French was limited to what I'd learned when I'd helped my former best friend Tindra cram for tests.

The guard raised the scanner. "Look straight ahead and don't blink for five seconds."

I obeyed. Seconds passed, and the scanner was taking longer to clear me than it had the others. The guard turned it toward her and examined it before pushing a few buttons.

"These portable scanners are junk." She held it up. "I need to rescan your eyes."

A few more seconds passed, and I forced myself to appear nonchalant. Finally, there was a beep, and the guard waved the scanner toward the plane door.

* * *

After we landed in the Atlantic Region, Tessa gave instructions while the plane entered a hangar. "We've made contact with our agent at the Zoo. He's here to escort you there. When you've obtained information on Jared Canton, contact Chad. I programmed his number into your courier."

"Okay," I said. The plane's engine shut down, and two cars drove into the hangar before the door closed.

Tessa guided us to the waiting cars. The drivers remained inside, but the trunks popped open. "Get in," she said. "These vehicles will take you to your destination. Agatha and I exchanged glances. "Move along. The ventilation is more than adequate."

We climbed inside, and as soon as I was enclosed, a light glimmered and air flowed. The ride was short, and soon we traveled across gravel and stopped. The trunk released, and a man with a neatly trimmed beard offered his hand.

"I'm Evan. Welcome to the Zoo."

The area was thickly wooded, and Evan had parked in front of a brick building. Next to us, the other driver helped Agatha from the trunk.

Evan led us toward the building. "We're actually on the grounds of an old wildlife preserve." He grinned. "When you go inside, you'll see where this place gets the name." He held out his hand. "I need your couriers for security reasons."

We surrendered them and entered the building that held a taxidermist's dream. All kinds of preserved animals decorated the room. Heads and antlers hung from walls. Full animal bodies posed in corners. Whoever had named this place the Zoo had a sick sense of humor. I shuddered, and when I looked at Agatha, she grinned.

I stared at a stuffed squirrel clutching a nut and wondered why it was necessary to do that to the poor animal.

"Welcome to the Zoo, ladies," a deep voice boomed.

I whirled around. It was Liam, Drake's brother.

He extended his hand to Agatha and introduced himself. "I'm the agent in charge of this camp. Let's have a seat." He pointed to a couch that was arranged against the wall opposite a twelve-point buck, and we sat. He remained standing.

"Is Ophelia okay?" I blurted.

"She left the Warehouse prior to the ambush." His stern expression relaxed. "Thanks for asking. Now, Agatha, we'll begin with you. When the attack occurred, you were about to be sent to the field."

"Yes."

"You're involved with Chad Yeats."

Agatha looked away from Liam's intense gaze. "Yes. But until today I had no idea—"

"We cooperate with European intelligence. Keep what you know to yourself."

"Yes sir." Agatha's curls bounced.

"Now, from what I've learned from Agent Portner—"

"Is he here?" I leaned forward, hoping he'd gone elsewhere.

"Yes. But I'd appreciate it if you'd allow me to address Agent Sparks without interruption."

I sat back with a scowl. He was as irritating as Drake.

"You said *agent.*" A smile broke on Agatha's face. "You're promoting me?"

"Effective immediately. Now, since I've got nothing else to add to that, if you'll excuse me, I'm going to check on your couriers to see if they've cleared security."

He left the room.

"Congratulations," I said. "Are you excited?"

"Nervous."

"Why? You're the one who led us out of the Warehouse during an attack."

"Yes, but I'm a lousy judge of character. I trusted Chad, and the whole time he was lying. We'd talked about getting married when the war is over."

"He was following orders," I said. "What if something happens, and you never see him again?"

"You don't understand how important honesty is to me." She crossed her arms and avoided my gaze.

Liam strode into the room and handed Agatha her courier. "I've downloaded the details of your first mission. Read them and be ready to go tomorrow morning."

"Thank you," Agatha said.

"All part of the job. Now, I'd like to speak to Miss Wilkins privately."

Agatha shot an encouraging smile in my direction before she hurried away.

Liam dragged a wooden chair across the room and straddled it. "I'll be blunt. We lost some outstanding prospective agents—"

"I know. It's my fault. If I hadn't let Drake take me to the Warehouse—"

"I thought I asked you not to interrupt me." His forehead creased.

"Sorry."

"Blaming anyone but our enemy is futile." He took my courier from his pocket and gave it to me. "With President Fortune's announcement about executing prisoners, we need people in the field. We're doing your eye surgery tonight so you can leave tomorrow morning."

I was afraid to ask about the polygraph. "You think I'm ready?"

"We're breaking up our training camps to avoid more ambushes." Liam cleared his throat. "Your training will continue in the field under Agent Sparks's supervision."

"Good." I tried not to let the enormous amount of relief show on my face.

"Drake found the reeducation center where Emma and Jesse Barry are being held. It's a boarding school. Agent Sparks will attempt to infiltrate in order to liberate all of the students. You'll help. The details are on your courier."

"But what about my mother? And Ben? Can't I be assigned to them?"

"Drake and I thought you'd be pleased with this assignment since you feel responsible for what happened to the Barry kids." He paused and rubbed the stubble on his chin. "Even though you're not."

"I do, but—"

"We're monitoring Ben and your mother. Neither one has been scheduled for execution. Yet."

How comforting. I sighed and scrolled through the courier, searching for the file that outlined my assignment. When I found the file, I opened it.

"Vivica, stop looking at the file and listen."

The urgency in his voice caused me to drop the courier in my lap. I met his blue eyes that were so much like his brother's.

"We gave you this assignment because it's a perfect fit for completing on-the-job training. Agatha will be in charge of the mission, and you'll help from the sidelines with technology."

I nodded.

"Look, you know I trust Drake with my life, right?"

"I figured as much."

"Whether you believe it or not, my brother is impressed with you."

I raised my eyebrows.

Liam grinned. "You annoy him, and he irritates you. But believe me, he never would've let you do all the things you've done for the Warriors if he thought you weren't capable. Read the details of your mission, and be ready to go."

When I left the room, I ran into Drake. I hadn't expected him to be here.

"I was coming to find you." His grim face caused my heart to seize. He put his hand on my shoulder and guided me into an empty lab. Jars containing specimens of preserved creatures lined the walls.

I turned away from them. "Did something happen to Ben?"

"No. Not everything revolves around Ben." His forehead creased just like his brother's. "Did Tessa ask you to make a bargain?"

I told him. "How'd you even know to ask?"

"Doesn't matter."

"Agatha told you." I scowled.

"Why'd you agree to Tessa's terms?"

"We were desperate. I never agreed to give Canton's location away. If the Europeans think he knows something, shouldn't we help them? It might affect us."

Drake crossed his arms. "So you're qualified to make that call?"

"What did you expect me to do?"

"Oh, I don't know. Contact me before making a deal?"

"I'm sorry. She caught me off guard. My training hasn't exactly been ideal. I spent about two weeks at training camp and have only read a field training manual. So if I'm not well-versed in protocol, you'll have to excuse me." I put my hands on my hips. "I don't get what the big deal is."

Drake ran his fingers through his hair, and the spikes stood at odd angles. "You've made an agreement with foreign intelligence, and they expect you to come through. And guess who has to handle it? I don't need that right now. You may be able to pull this kind of stunt with Ben, and he'll go along with your whims, but I—"

"Why would you think this has anything to do with Ben?"

"To you, everything does, doesn't it?"

That was so unfair. I bit back a curse and forced myself to take a deep breath. "Drake,

I—"

"It would be best if you addressed me as Agent Freeman from now on."

"Why?"

"Because I'm your superior. And you seem to forget that. Now you were saying?"

I took a step back and looked at my feet. I'd wanted to apologize, but that desire had fled. "Have you considered sending me to talk to Canton so I can keep my end of the bargain, *Agent Freeman*?"

He scowled. "That's not where we need you right now, which is the whole point. Besides, you haven't even finished your training."

"Give me time. I'll make this right."

"You will. But you can do it with another supervisor."

CHAPTER 10

The drugs the eye doctor had given me swept away my anxiety over arguing with Drake. I relaxed in the chair and watched Dr. Park prepare to inject nanobots into my vitreous gel. They would change my retina to match my new identity. Then, she'd inject pigment into my iris so my aquamarine eyes would become hazel.

"I have one question for you," Dr. Park said. She was a pretty Asian woman whose lab coat had an eyeball-pattern. "Would you be willing to participate in a study?"

I giggled. "Shouldn't you have asked me that before drugging me?"

"Yes, I apologize. I would like to insert a lens that contains a recording device behind your iris. Whatever you see, the Panorama Lens will capture."

"No way…that's creepy."

"It would only record when you activate it using a code. Panorama could be quite beneficial to you as an agent. Of course, we can remove it at any time and can never use it to spy on you."

That was kind of cool. "Okay, go for it."

She patted my arm. "Sit back and relax. I'm going to begin now."

My mind drifted to the lake where my mother and I had

vacationed the summer before my life had turned upside down. Soothing water lapped against my raft as it bobbed in the lake. The sun warmed me.

Then my thoughts floated to Isaac. Was he okay? Did he have Ben's brown eyes? When I'd left Isaac, his eyes seemed like they might darken.

Did Ben ever think of me while he waited in prison? Were the Warriors planning to rescue him? Would they be willing to save my mother too?

A wave of pain threatened to submerge my peaceful drifting. The water, which had been serene, was now choppy and dark. Why did thinking of my mother have to wreck my dream?

I wanted to forget, but I couldn't.

From a distant shore, I heard a calming voice. "We're all done, Vivica."

* * *

The next day, Liam arranged a flight to the city in the Atlantic Region where Emma and Jesse's boarding school was located. Only hours later, wearing our disguises, Agatha and I climbed aboard and discussed mission details in the air.

There was a job-opening at the school for a dorm supervisor, and Agatha had applied using her alias. She'd interview with the headmaster tomorrow morning while I worked from a safe house near the school.

Agatha rested her courier in her lap. "You'd rather be the one on the inside, wouldn't you?"

"Yes. I love Emma and Jesse. Their mother and father helped me when I needed it."

"You can trust me," she said.

It wasn't like I had a choice, but she'd been a good friend so far.

I hoped that boded well for our mission. "What made you want to join the Emancipation Warriors?"

"I spent my teenage years at the Great Plains Academy for Children and Young Adults—a fancy name for a reeducation center."

I cringed. "I'm sorry."

Agatha stared out the jet's window. "Six years ago, the police arrested my parents for violating the Peace and Unity Act. Someone came up with evidence that proved they were participating in anti-government activity."

"Who turned them in?"

"Our neighbor." Agatha's face bent into a scowl. "She was like a grandma to me. I trusted her. She baked cookies for us. Babysat my brother and me. Taught me to knit. And she betrayed all of us. When my brother and I were being put in the car to go to the reeducation center, she had the nerve to cry and tell me she was sorry. She was doing her patriotic duty."

"Wow." No wonder Agatha was so angry with Chad for lying about his identity.

"She felt so guilty that she needed to get it off of her chest." Agatha paused for a few seconds. "When you're thirteen and see something like that happen to your parents, you realize what they're fighting for matters. I made up my mind that I'd play the government's reeducation game. And when I turned eighteen, and it was time for me to be released into society, I'd use everything I'd learned against the government."

"That's how you ended up at the Warehouse and why you changed your name?"

She hesitated. "Pretty much."

"And your parents are still in prison?"

She nodded.

I rested my hand on her shoulder. She'd been so quick to think of me when President Fortune had announced the execution of prisoners, but her family was in danger too. "What happened to your brother?"

Tears welled in Agatha's eyes. "He's sixteen. So he's still being reeducated."

* * *

The next morning I'd finished breakfast in an Atlantic Region safe house when my courier dinged. It was a message from Agatha. During her interview, she'd sneaked a picture of the list of names, numbers and addresses of the next two women being evaluated for the female dorm manager's position at the Atlantic Academy.

`You know what to do. :)`

The next interview was at 10:15. I glanced at my watch—9:36.

That wasn't a lot of time, but I'd have to make something work. I put on a pair of walking shoes and grabbed a jacket. Rummaging through the case of tools we'd brought with us, I selected a few and stuffed them in my jacket pockets. Agatha had our car, so I'd be forced to walk a half mile to the home of the target, Elena Velazquez.

The morning was sunny and brisk, so I covered the distance quickly. The sidewalk was uneven on the street of government houses. Each of the cottages was small and gray with stark black numbers on white doors.

I slowed when I approached 1058.

A teal hatchback was parked in the driveway next to the cottage.

My hand closed around the device in my pocket that looked like a rock. When I got close to the car, I let the rock drop from my pocket. While I moved forward, I kicked the rock, and it skittered under the car.

Perfect shot.

I glanced at my watch and picked up my pace. It was 9:50, and I assumed Elena would try to leave home and arrive at the interview early. I ducked behind a tree and used my courier as a remote control.

With the press of a few buttons, I transformed the rock underneath Elena's car into a tiny robot. When it was touching the tire, I fired a needle, and it bored into the car's left rear tire. Since time was running out, I moved the robot and made a second gouge. The tire needed to be flat when she came out of her house.

I shifted the device away from the car and turned it back into a rock. Pretending to drop my sunglasses, I scooped up the rock and glasses and fled down the street to the safe house.

* * *

Last night after we had arrived, I'd started working on hacking the Atlantic Academy's network. I'd made progress, enough to monitor incoming calls. So, when I returned to the safe house, I plopped on the couch and prepared to intercept Elena's call.

It was 10:03. I prayed I hadn't missed it.

I busied myself by continuing to try to gain access to their network, because that would be the best way to prevent the next interview, and it would keep me from having to run all over the entire city.

My screen flashed with an incoming call from Elena's number. "Atlantic Academy. How may I direct your call?"

"Please, I must speak to Mr. Geissler."

"He's conducting an interview. May I take a message?"

"Yes. I am supposed to have an interview at 10:15, but I have a flat tire. I cannot be there on time."

"I'm very sorry. Would you like to reschedule for tomorrow?"

"I would be grateful."

"How about 1:45 tomorrow afternoon?"

"Yes, thank you."

When I disconnected the call, I bit my lip. I was responsible for ruining this poor woman's day. She probably needed the money.

But we were at war.

Agatha burst through the safe house door. "I nailed my interview. Did you stop the other candidates?"

I told her about Elena. "I'm working on the 11:15 interview." It was easier for me to think about a time slot rather than a person. "We have to let that interview happen, but when Mr. Geissler calls references, I'm going to be ready to give a bad one."

"Cool."

* * *

The next afternoon Agatha and I were listening to the news when her government-issued doc buzzed. It was registered to her alias, Betty Claymore. Agatha's eyes widened. "It's Mr. Geissler." She answered and listened. When she turned her back, my heart sank.

She disconnected and faced me. "I didn't get the job." She rubbed the back of her neck.

"How is that even possible?" My eyes widened.

"I have no idea. He said I wasn't a good fit—none of the candidates have been." She scowled. "He was rambling about how one woman missed her interview yesterday and then showed up unexpectedly today."

Poor Elena.

"I don't get it," Agatha said. "With all the sabotage, I should've been the obvious choice."

"Now what?"

"Well…" She hesitated. "Looks like I'm going to have to send you to try."

Chapter 11

Agatha prepped me for Fredrica Lloyd's afternoon interview at Atlantic Academy the next day. As soon as we'd learned Agatha was out of the running, we said some desperate prayers and submitted Fredrica's application. A couple of hours later, Abelard Geissler called and requested an interview.

My courier buzzed, but it was a number I didn't recognize.

"Agent Wilkins."

"*Miss* Wilkins, it's Agent Portner, and 'til you earn it, don't you dare call yourself an agent. Got it?"

I gritted my teeth. "Yes sir. What can I do for you, sir?"

"I'm in charge of you now, since Agent Freeman is sick of dealing with your shenanigans."

I closed my eyes. Was I that bad? I hadn't thought Drake would follow through with his threat.

"What's the deal with your current project?"

He wasn't going to like my news. "Um…well…" I waved my hand to get Agatha's attention and mouthed that it was Jethro.

"Spit it out."

"Agent Sparks and I—"

Agatha snatched the courier from my hand, changed the call to video mode, and projected Jethro's image onto the wall. "I'd like to explain, sir."

"Go ahead." His jaws attacked his gum.

She told him about all that had happened. When she finished, Jethro was silent for a moment.

"That's a big risk, Agent Sparks. If this don't work, I'll hold you personally responsible and yank you both out of the field."

Behind my back, I gathered a fistful of my shirt. I'd probably ruin everything for both of us.

"I understand, sir."

"If there's a miracle, and Miss Wilkins somehow gets offered the job and manages to get better results than her last poly, then your career won't be toast."

My shoulders drooped. Why would he tell me this now instead of letting me believe I had a chance? Maybe we should forget the whole thing. There had to be another way to rescue the children.

Agatha's chin raised slightly. "I believe in her."

"Glad there's one of us."

She disconnected the call and handed the courier back to me. "Don't let him get to you."

"Thank you." I hesitated and tried to read her expression that didn't seem as confident as it had when she'd faced Jethro. "We don't have to do this."

"Yes, I do. *We* do." She put her hands on her hips.

"You heard him."

"Jethro's opinion doesn't matter." She pushed up her sleeves. "With God, all things are possible."

"Then we'd better start praying."

* * *

Mr. Abelard Geissler looked like Santa Claus must have when he was a young man. If Santa had ever been thirty years old, lacked a beard, and worn a tie with cartoon characters. I shook Mr. Geissler's clammy hand and perched in the seat in front of his desk while I willed my stomach to stop churning. I adjusted my lavender cardigan and smoothed my calf-length, flowered skirt.

Fredrica's taste in clothing was horrible.

He scrolled through his MD3. "Now, I know your application is here somewhere. If I can find it, we'll be good to go. Give me a minute." His device buzzed, and Fredrica's doc vibrated in my pocket. "Oh, darn. Now I'll never find what I'm looking for.

I removed the doc. A message from the government's new notification system had overridden both of our docs, and until we viewed the video message, the docs wouldn't perform other functions.

I smiled. "I guess we have to listen." I pressed start, and it synced with Mr. Geissler's MD3.

"Attention citizens of the United Regions of North America, President Fortune is pleased to announce the destruction of a rebel training camp known as the Zoo." Footage of the familiar brick building, now crumbled and smoldering, displayed on the screen. I stifled a gasp. "It's unknown how many rebels were killed in this raid, but President Fortune expresses his confidence that this will be a blow to the rebels' morale and that the war will end soon."

I said a silent prayer of thanks that the training camp had been closed and that this message was more theater from the government. "That's good news."

"Certainly is." Mr. Geissler swiped his MD3. "Give me a minute to try to find that file."

"No problem."

"There it is." Mr. Geissler's eyes twinkled. "Finally. That was painful. Now, Ms. Lloyd, what makes you want to work at the Atlantic Academy?"

I smiled and met his gaze. "I love children. I've wanted to work with them since I was a little girl, and then there was my sister..." I paused for a second and allowed tears to pool in my eyes. "Rebels killed my little sister Hannah a few years ago." My voice broke. "I can't bear the thought of that happening to more children. I want to be part of teaching our children peace and unity. I'm not tough enough to be on the front lines of this battle. But...but I can do my part here, helping kids understand the government is for our good and protection." I blinked and allowed tears to streak my face.

Mr. Geissler shot from his desk and stumbled to a shelf that held a box of recycled tissues. He shoved it toward me. I clutched the soft cloth, dabbed my tears, and pretended to fight for my composure. "I'm so sorry."

"Don't apologize." He fidgeted with his MD3. "We, uh, can move on."

I sniffed. "Thank you."

"Now can you tell me why you're qualified for this job?"

"Of course. I have a bachelor's degree in early childhood education with a minor in psychology. My background would be helpful in dealing with children who've come from difficult circumstances and need help adjusting."

"Yes, we often see that here, I'm afraid. I think of myself as a father figure to these lost souls whose parents have brainwashed them."

"I'm sure that's something they all need," I paused. "I'm also fluent in Spanish and Mandarin."

"That's quite impressive."

"Thank you." My former nanny, Ana, had taught me Spanish, and my mother had forced me to take Mandarin lessons.

He put on a pair of round, wire rimmed glasses and perused my application. "What are your strengths and weaknesses?"

"I'm very organized. That's a strength, but it can also be a weakness because it means I tend to be very task oriented. Working with children would give me the chance to improve, because with children, you must be flexible." I forced a sheepish smile. "I'm really bad with computers. They totally hate me."

Mr. Geissler smiled and leaned forward. "I understand. Computers hate me too. It must have been wonderful to live in the days of unrestricted paper use." He waved his MD3 and removed his glasses. "As for your other weakness, I understand that too. This morning, I was on my way to interviews when a group of kids stopped me. They wanted me to look at the paintings they'd been working on in art class. Even though it made me late, I had to stop and look."

"Instances like that, no doubt, make you an excellent headmaster."

I cringed inwardly. That was way too thick.

But Mr. Geissler beamed, and his cheeks flushed. "Thank you. I have to check your references, but I'm going to call our polygraph examiner. I'd like you to go ahead and take the test."

"Wow. That's wonderful." My stomach rolled.

He adjusted his tie. "I hope you do well, because I'd love to have you on board."

* * *

An elevator next to Mr. Geissler's office led to a lower level, where cheerful yellow walls decorated with student artwork paved the way to the polygraph room. I tried not to dwell on what was riding on this test, but each reason mocked me. Emma and Jesse. Agatha's career. Proving myself so I could help Ben and my mother.

With God, all things are possible.

The familiar glass and metal tube stood in the middle of the room, so I headed inside and placed my feet on the footprints and prayed the tips Agatha had given me would work. I reviewed the details of Fredrica Lloyd's life. Or, as I needed to be thinking of it, my life.

The door swung open, and a tall man who was in his early twenties strolled in and sat at the table. He had a confident air, and though his nose was a bit too big, he was still handsome with brown eyes that reminded me of Ben's.

"Good afternoon. I'm sorry for making you wait." He had a touch of a French accent.

He wasn't sorry, but I smiled. "I don't mind. I want this job because I love kids."

He flashed a smile that didn't reach his eyes. "My name is Jean. I will be administering your polygraph test today. Please relax."

He pushed some buttons, and the cap descended from the machine and dangled above my head. "One more thing." He opened a drawer and retrieved a plastic container. Popping the lid, he dumped a small metal disk into his hand. "Fasten this to the back side of your upper teeth." He extended his hand.

I frowned and took the disk. "What's it for?"

"Some people try to fool polygraphs by biting their tongues. This sensor will detect that nonsense."

My stomach roiled. "Oh." I faked a smile and fastened the disk to the back of my mouthpiece. Physical tricks were off the table. What else did the Warriors not know about?

Please God, keep me calm enough to pass this.

The machine sprang to life, and after a routine stim test and round of probable lie questions, the interrogation intensified.

"Are you a loyal citizen of the United Regions of North America?"

I focused on my happy memories of Ben. "Yes."

"Are you involved in activities that violate the Peace and Unity Act or could be considered treasonous?"

I pictured the first time Ben and I had smiled at each other during URNA history. "No."

"Are you willing to report any suspicious activity to your superiors?"

"Yes." Just not the superiors he meant.

"Are you loyal to President Fortune?"

"Yes." Loyally committed to taking him down.

Jean showered me with questions for an hour, and I prayed that the interview would end soon. My feet and legs ached, and I rubbed my lower back.

"Do you believe the government has a right to destroy citizens when the evidence is clear they've participated in activities deemed unlawful, dangerous, and a threat to the peace of our nation?"

In light of the president's recent announcement, this question chilled me. "Yes."

Jean took a moment to study his computer screen before he looked up. "We're finished, Ms. Lloyd. Mr. Geissler will contact you."

CHAPTER 12

I paced the safe house while I waited for Mr. Geissler's call.

"I'm sure you did fine," Agatha said from the couch, where she sat knitting. "Why don't you try to think about something else? Like Ben."

I grinned.

"Made you smile," she said. "By the way, I'm shocked that Drake dumped you."

"He asked for me to be assigned to a different supervisor. There's a difference."

"Right. Whatever you say."

Speaking of Drake…I pulled the courier from my pocket and dialed his number. There was something I needed to know.

It rang several times before he answered. "So, my dear, you heard the news, I take it."

"Agent Freeman, if we're going to be more formal with each other, then I'm not your *dear.*"

"Okay, *sweetie.*"

I gritted my teeth. "You're such a jerk."

"And you're a spoiled brat."

"I was planning to leave a message."

"And I nearly let you. But there was no point in delaying this inevitable confrontation. I just thought you should know, requesting your reassignment wasn't an easy decision for me, but it's in everyone's best interest."

"Or it was the result of an impulsive threat that you had to follow through on so you could prove you're stronger than Ben when it comes to dealing with me."

Silence.

Drake always had a retort. What was wrong with him? "Never mind. Did you tell Jethro about my deal with the Europeans?"

"No. But keep pushing me, and I might."

"What should I do?"

He sighed. "I'll contact you when I find Canton and see if we can arrange a meet."

"Thank you."

"Given Jethro's opinion of you, I'd highly recommend keeping this to yourself." He disconnected, and I stared at the courier. When I looked up, Agatha was gazing at me.

"What?"

"Nothing." She looked down at the hat she was making.

"You have an opinion."

Across the room, Fredrica's government-issued doc chimed. "You'd better get that." Her eyes rested on the device.

"And after I do, I want to know what you're thinking." I ran to answer.

"Fredrica? Abelard Geissler here. I'd like to offer you the job."

My legs weakened. *Thank you, God!* "That's wonderful. When can I start?"

* * *

A week later, Mr. Geissler guided me down a sidewalk that led to the girls' dormitory at Atlantic Academy. It was a sunny morning, and my first day as the headmistress of the girls' dorm. We arrived at a red brick building where Mr. Geissler opened the door.

"Thank you, Mr. Geissler."

"Call me Abelard, please."

I smiled. "Of course."

The lobby was spacious with groups of couches and chairs arranged for socializing. I smelled cookies baking.

"Is there a kitchen nearby?"

Abelard pointed across the lobby. "Over there. Around the corner is a community kitchen. The oven is small, but some of the older kids use it all the time."

A teenage girl wearing a uniform sat at the front desk. "Hi, Mr. Geissler."

"Good morning, Lilly. How are you?"

She smiled robotically. "Fantastic."

Abelard walked to a door off of the lobby, swiped a key pad with his MD3, stood aside, and motioned for me to enter. "Your new abode."

The tiny apartment had an open floor plan with a kitchenette. From the front door, I could see the bedroom and the bathroom off of the living room that was painted a soothing pale green. A worn beige couch and chair furnished the living room.

"It's great. Much more spacious than my college dorm."

Abelard laughed. "These aren't deluxe accommodations, but I'm sure you're glad you don't have to pay for housing out of your salary."

"Definitely."

"I'll leave you alone." He fished an MD3 from his pocket. "You get the big-girl toys now that you work for the government. You'll find it's quite the upgrade from your doc." I took it. "Has a tutorial with step by step instructions for people like you and me. And you can find a list of the girls who live in this dorm in the student management program. That's all for now. Call me if you need anything."

* * *

As soon as Abelard left, I swept the apartment for bugs. When the room came up clean, I took a look at the MD3 and browsed the list of girls who lived in the dorm. There were a few four-year-olds, which was the age Emma and Jesse were, because they were the youngest children the school tried to reeducate. The government placed children younger than age four in state-approved foster homes.

When I examined records, I stumbled upon the school's handbook. I opened the file and read for a while. Most four-year-olds didn't need to stay at the reeducation centers for very long because they were easier to brainwash. The manual didn't use those words, but that was my interpretation. Ideally, they liked to keep small children for less than a year before placing them into an adoptive home.

If they were brought to the reeducation center before age sixteen, they could stay until age eighteen. Anyone over age sixteen caught violating the Peace and Unity Act was treated as an adult and sent to prison.

After searching the records of all the four-year-old students, I identified Emma and Jesse from the pictures included in the files. The twins had been given new names—Mia and Caden. According to the documents, a couple was already interested in adopting them, and because of this couple's high rank in the government and the children's ages, they'd be eligible in two weeks.

* * *

Lilly was working the front desk when I came out of my apartment. I walked over and extended my hand. "Lilly, I'm Miss Lloyd."

She smiled. "Welcome."

"How long have you lived here?"

She paused as if searching for the answer. "Six years. I came when I was ten."

"What do you like about living here?"

"Everyone is so nice. We have fun activities. I like everything we learn in our classes too. My friends are great."

I forced a smile. It was obvious why they had Lilly working the front desk. "I'm going to explore."

I left the dorm and headed for the three-story building that Abelard had indicated was used for classes.

The first floor was for the youngest children. When I came to a classroom, I found a room full of children who appeared to be ages four to six. Emma and Jesse sat in a circle with the other children. I hovered outside the door, pressed my hand to my heart, and studied the little boy and girl who looked even more like their mother than I'd remembered. If I hadn't come into their lives…

But I had. And that's why I was here. To make things right.

The young teacher read a book about different kinds of families and how not every family needed to have only one mommy and daddy. Some had five mommies and one daddy. Or three mommies. Or two daddies.

I cringed, knowing how Judd and Monica would feel about this story, but it wasn't unlike the books my teachers had read to me when I was growing up.

I moved on to the next classroom where some older children practiced multiplication tables. When I went upstairs, the middle school students were reading novels silently, and the high school students on the third floor were listening to a lecture on the benefits of a command economy.

If the Emancipation Warriors had identified this school as a reeducation center, then I still wasn't seeing how it was different from other schools, except that students lived here full time.

There had to be more below the surface.

* * *

When I was safely back in my apartment, I called Agatha. "I'm missing something."

"I know. You're just *now* figuring it out?" She giggled.

"Thanks. But seriously, I need your advice. I roamed the halls of the school, and I didn't hear any more propaganda than what I grew up with in my regular school. Is there more?"

Agatha cleared her throat. "Oh, yeah. Keep digging. These reeducation centers do put on a great show. The kids seem happy, but..."

"But what?"

"Look through your files. Is there anybody new? An older student."

I opened the files on the MD3 and projected them. "Yeah. Paige Andrews. Age thirteen. Brought in three days ago."

"Perfect. Is there any other information in her file?"

"Her parents were arrested. Suspected rebels." As I said the words, I hated how familiar and painful they would probably be to Agatha.

But she didn't hesitate. "Find her. Befriend her. Get her to tell you all the things they're doing to her, because I guarantee you she's not in the classroom yet."

My stomach turned. "Where is she?"

"She's being reeducated."

* * *

I knocked and waited outside room 218 a few days later. I'd meant to check sooner, but I'd been busy with some of the younger girls who needed a lot of my attention.

I tapped the door again. "Paige?"

The door cracked open, and a girl with short, ratted hair peered through the opening. "What?"

"I'm Miss Lloyd. I'm in charge of the dorm."

"That's nice." Paige started to slam the door, but I blocked it with my foot.

"Wait. May I talk to you? Since you arrived last week, I wanted to make sure you're okay."

"You're just now checking? I'm fine."

Agatha would've been better at this, but I pressed ahead. "If you ever want to talk, you're welcome in my apartment downstairs."

"I know where it is." Paige opened the door a bit more and revealed the purple shadows under her eyes. "You don't have to be nice to me. I'm not going to fall for the good cop act."

Good cop? Then that meant she'd met a bad cop. I shifted. "I'll let you get some rest."

Paige reached up to close the door, and I gasped at the bruise that encircled her wrist. I started to touch her arm, but she jerked away.

"How'd that happen?"

Paige scowled. "Like you don't know."

"I don't."

Her frown relaxed, and she looked into my eyes. Suspicion dawned in hers as she studied me, but then her expression hardened again. "I don't care what they do to me, but I'm going to say this anyway." She lifted her chin. "And you can report me."

"Maybe you shouldn't—"

"If you don't know what the people who run this place do in the basement of the infirmary, then you'd better find out quick. Because I wouldn't want to be standing in your shoes on Judgment Day."

Paige slammed the door, and I vowed to make a trip to the infirmary basement that night.

CHAPTER 13

Prior to exploring the infirmary basement, I had to hack into the Atlantic Academy's security system, so I wouldn't be caught on camera snooping. I made some adjustments so the cameras ran on recorded footage instead of a live feed and headed out, dressed in my jogging clothes. I made a loop around the campus in case anyone was watching, but in the middle of my second round, I detoured toward the back entrance of the infirmary.

The door required a pass code, which I'd unearthed earlier. I typed the numbers and heard a metallic click. The door led into a stairwell, and I hurried to the basement, where I encountered a second door with a pass code. I punched it in and found myself in a narrow hall illuminated by fluorescent lights and lined with grimy subway tiles.

I tiptoed so the rubber soles of my shoes wouldn't squeak on the tile floor. When I came to a door, I peeked through the window. It was a room with an empty hospital bed, but the sheets and blankets were disheveled.

I continued and found a few more doors that led to empty rooms with smooth sheets and blankets on beds.

The next room was a lab. My hand flew to my mouth. Paige was restrained and hooked up to monitors. A short man with stringy hair and a pock-marked face sat at a computer next to the table where Paige lay. I flattened myself against the wall next to the door to listen.

"Who was your parents' contact in the Emancipation Warriors?"

"My parents were loyal citizens of the United Regions of North America."

The man typed something into his computer, and a few seconds later, I heard a buzz. Paige screamed, and her entire body lurched.

"Do you care to answer that again?"

"Like I've answered the last five times?"

"Fine. We'll try something different. Do you agree to be a loyal citizen of the United Regions of North America? Do you agree to obey all laws and recognize President Fortune as the supreme authority?"

Supreme authority? That was a new line that made me long for a barf bag.

"Never."

When the machine buzzed, Paige cried out, but it was muffled, like she was trying to fight the pain.

"I'll ask you again." He stood, adjusted his stained lab coat, and leered over her. "And I'd like to tell you what happens to nice little girls who refuse to be reeducated."

Bile rose in my throat. Horror splayed over Paige's face, but she lifted her chin. "What's that?"

"You're young. You're pretty." He stroked her face. "And you'd bring a nice high price at an auction full of men who like to have a good time with your type. We can always use you again and again to bring in money to help defeat your parents in their pathetic little rebellion."

The terror resurfaced on Paige's face. She was about to break. I pushed up my sleeves.

"You're going to tell me that you're loyal to President Fortune. And after that, you're going to tell me everything your parents and their rebel friends knew. Understand?"

Her eyes widened, and her posture stiffened.

I almost sprang from my hiding place to kill the sick-o with my bare hands. But even though Dr. Pervert was shorter than me, he was probably stronger, and I had to get Paige out without blowing my cover. I pulled my courier from my pocket and sent a text to Agatha.

`Student being tortured. Infirmary basement. Extraction. NOW!`

God, please show me how to help this girl. I ducked, so I couldn't be seen through the window on the door, and found a closet. It opened easily and was full of medicines. Examining the bottles, I chose one I recognized as a sedative. The time I'd spent reading while I was pregnant and hiding out had paid off.

I yanked open a drawer, searching for a syringe. It took several tries, but I found a new one. After filling the syringe with the sedative, I returned to the lab door and moved out of sight.

I glanced at my courier. Agatha had replied.

`On my way.`

Dr. Pervert had his back to the door. I tossed the empty sedative bottle on the floor, and it clattered and rolled away. The man strode toward the lab door and pushed it open. I caught him in a headlock, jammed the syringe in his neck, and pushed.

He struggled for a few seconds before he collapsed. Paige started to shake and cry as I unhooked the restraints. "Who are you? I thought…"

"I'm with the Warriors."

I unfastened the last of the restraints, and when Paige stepped off the table, her knees buckled. Putting an arm around her shoulder, I held her up and guided her out of the lab.

"I—I have to tell you something," Paige said.

"Can it wait?" We shuffled to the door.

She shook her head. "My parents found out something about the government. I didn't tell the doctor. I made something up so he'd leave me alone. President Fortune is making some kind of deal with the Council of World Peacekeepers. Something to do with a city in the Republic of Asia."

I stopped. "What kind of deal?"

She trembled. "I don't know, but it's important. I overheard my mom and dad talking. My dad knew a guy who worked for European intelligence, and they were trying to figure out what to do right before they died last week. I didn't know who to tell."

"Can you remember anything else?"

"No. They didn't talk about it in front of me. I'm sorry."

I hugged her. "Don't be. You've been a big help." I called Agatha. "Where are you?"

"At the corner of Main and Second."

Paige's weight slumped against me while I hoisted her up the stairs. "You can't stay there. Traffic cams." I wiped my brow with my shoulder.

"I know," Agatha said. "What about the park across from the Academy campus?"

I paused on the landing to catch my breath. If we could get out the infirmary door, we'd have to cross the street to get to the park. "Fine." I disconnected the call. "Stay with me, Paige. We're almost there."

She collapsed, and I caught her head before it slammed against the concrete.

"God, please," I said. We'd made it to the last locked door. I punched in the pass code, and when it swung open, the man who'd given me my polygraph test blocked it.

CHAPTER 14

My heart plummeted before it started racing. I swung at Jean's face, but he caught my wrist.

"My dear, I wouldn't do that if I were you." The French accent was gone.

"Cavalier?" I whispered. He'd given me the polygraph? No wonder I'd passed. It didn't say a lot about the organization's faith in me, but I stored that thought away to deal with later.

"What're you doing?" he whispered. "This isn't part of your mission."

"Moonbeam's on her way."

Drake pulled a black mask over his face and scooped Paige up, obstructing her face with his chest. "Where's she meeting you?"

"The park across the street."

I started to follow Drake out the door.

"I don't think so." He blocked my path. "Stay here. Erase security cam footage. Moonbeam and I will take care of Paige."

I bit my lip. "Call me when she's safe."

He nodded and disappeared into the darkness.

* * *

I jogged back to my apartment and checked the security and traffic cameras three times to make sure I hadn't missed anything. A few minutes after I'd finished, someone pounded on my door.

"Fredrica? Open up. It's urgent!" Abelard yelled.

I kicked off my shoes, threw a robe on over my clothes, and opened the door. "What's going on?"

"We have an emergency. There was a major security breach tonight. One of our students esc—er, ran away."

I gasped. "How? Is this my fault?" I allowed a note of panic to creep into my voice.

Abelard rested a hand on my arm. "No, no. This young lady was in the infirmary. There was nothing you could've done."

"How can I help?"

"Do a room check. The missing girl is Paige Andrews, so of course she won't be there. But everyone else should be." He hurried away.

I accessed the student roster on my MD3 and did the room check.

* * *

After I reported to Abelard that the other girls were in their rooms, he assured me I could go to bed. We'd have a staff meeting tomorrow.

A few minutes after I'd dropped into bed, Drake called.

"Paige is okay. Moonbeam's taking care of her."

"Good." When would things be normal again with Drake? We might argue, but I'd at least considered him a friend. Now he was just one of my superiors. I passed along the information Paige had told me.

"And you couldn't get anything else out of her?"

"No. But she thought it was important."

"Could be. Fortune's always been friendly with the Peacekeepers. I'll see if I hear anything else."

There was more I needed to say. "I know you're mad at me, but

I'm sorry. I'm trying to do better, especially now that I'm a Christian. If I'd known the deal I made with the Europeans would upset you this much—"

"Finish this mission, and I'll get you to Canton."

Chapter 15

Abelard cleared his throat and fiddled with his MD3. "Good morning, everyone. I'm afraid we'll have to deviate from the agenda I sent yesterday afternoon. And to think I actually made an agenda for once. But after last night, well, there are too many things we need to discuss, and I…"

Abelard babbled for the next few minutes. The staff was gathered in the conference room in the administrative offices of the Atlantic Academy. Though there were ten people in the meeting, including Abelard and me, the only people I'd met were the men on my right and left. The man on my right had a bald spot but sported thick tufts of hair on the sides of his head. His name was Jake, and he was head of the boys' dorm. Don, on my left, wore a bow tie. He was principal of the middle school and high school.

Don tapped his stylus against the table, and Jake leaned back in his chair and crossed his arms. I hoped Abelard picked up on their cues soon, but I took a moment to glance at my MD3 to see if there was anything urgent. There wasn't.

"Now," Abelard said and paused to scroll through his MD3.

Jake sat up, and Don stopped tapping. I shoved my MD3 in my pocket.

"Due to the breach last night, we're going to have a visit this afternoon from some government officials. Unfortunately, it reflects badly on us when one of our charges manages to drug a doctor and get away."

A few of the women at the table gasped.

"Is the doctor okay?" one of them asked.

"Yes, yes. He's groggy since a large dose of sedative was used to incapacitate him, but we expect him to make a full recovery. He doesn't remember a thing, and no one can figure out how this girl managed to drug him and escape."

If they only knew.

Don twirled his stylus. "How do we know she didn't have help?"

"We suspect she did since her parents were high-ranking rebels, and our security camera footage shows nothing," Abelard said. "Which is why the government officials are coming to investigate. Oh, and by the way, this is our newest employee, Fredrica Lloyd." He motioned toward me. "I should've introduced her before I began the meeting, but I've had so much on my mind. She's in charge of the female dorm. Now, back to what I was saying. You have to understand how the rebels think. They truly believe they're—"

"Abelard, we don't want a dissertation on rebel beliefs. Just tell us what you need." Jake crossed his arms again.

Wow. That was harsh. I gave Abelard an encouraging smile.

Abelard's cheeks reddened. "Cooperation. If these officials want to ask questions, answer them. If they want to give you a polygraph, take it. If they want to see records, show them. Obviously, our full cooperation will go a long way with putting us back in the government's good graces. Please try to relax. I mean, these things happen—they've just never happened here on my watch, so I…"

I tuned Abelard out. Government officials paying the school a visit would definitely complicate our liberation mission.

* * *

During my afternoon break, I made a quick stop at the safe house while out on a grocery run. Agatha was curled up in a chair, knitting a teal scarf.

"The situation doesn't look good," I said. "If they suspect we've infiltrated, then we have to act soon. I'm new, so they'll look at me first. Plus, Emma and Jesse could be put up for adoption in less than a week."

"I'll talk to Drake about it tonight when he gets back from taking Paige to her foster family." Agatha stopped and put the scarf in her lap. "He's cool to work with. What do you know about his ex-girlfriend?"

Our operation was in serious jeopardy, and all she cared about was Drake's ex? I shook my head. "My encounters with Faith were nasty. I never figured out what Drake saw in her. Have you heard from Chad?"

Agatha's knitting needles clicked. Maybe I shouldn't have asked. She stretched out the scarf to survey her progress before she looked up.

"He's on some joint mission between the Europeans and Warriors, working on something with a hydrogen power plant, and won't be back for a while. And I'm okay with that. I don't know if I can trust him again."

"Don't you think you're being too hard on him? He was following orders."

"He lied."

"His accent is hot."

"You mean the accent I didn't know he had?" She rolled her eyes. "It's time to move on. There are other guys."

Like Drake. I studied Agatha as she wound yarn around her

finger. They'd make a good couple.

She stopped twisting the yarn. "Do you ever wonder if you can really trust anyone?"

"All the time."

"Then why do I want to keep trying?"

* * *

A few days later, I'd finished putting away my groceries when Fredrica's MD3 rang. "Fredrica, this is Abelard. May I see you in my office? There's an official here from the government."

I knocked away the dread and made my voice sound pleasant. "Absolutely."

The waiting room outside of Abelard's office was empty except for Jake. Abelard's door was closed, and his secretary, Wava, was gone.

"Have a seat," Jake said. "Wava's being questioned."

"How long have you been here?"

Jake glanced at his watch. "Twenty minutes or so. I'm ready to get this over with."

Abelard's secretary exited, and her complexion was pallid. She eased into her chair. "Jake, go on in."

After he went into the office and closed the door, I moved to the chair closest to her desk. "Are you okay?"

She emitted a shaky laugh. "The questioning was intense. Like I was guilty."

"But everybody's being interrogated, right?"

"Yes," Wava whispered. "I can't say any more. The official warned me not to."

Of course. I smiled and started to move back to my seat when a flyer on Wava's desk caught my attention because information printed on paper was so rare. I pointed to it. "May I see that?"

"Sure." Her expression brightened, and she handed it to me. "It's for a government-sponsored circus that's coming to town this weekend. I'm taking my son."

I finished reading the information, and an idea took root. I held out the flyer.

Wava held up her hand. "Keep it. I have another."

I stuffed it in my pocket. "Thanks."

Fifteen minutes later, Jake sauntered out of Abelard's office. "Your turn."

I started to enter Abelard's office and caught a glimpse of a woman with short, closely cropped black hair. I froze. Her head was bent, and she was studying something on her MD3, but I'd know that profile anywhere.

Martina Ward.

CHAPTER 16

I thanked God Martina had been looking down when I entered the office because the surprise displayed in my expression would've blown my cover. I prayed my disguise was as good as we'd all thought.

Questions pinged through my brain. Why would a woman who worked for the president bother with a reeducation center's problems? Had they somehow traced me again?

"Fredrica?" she said. "Close the door and sit." She pointed at the chair.

"Yes ma'am."

When I was seated, she stared into my eyes for a few seconds. I smiled wanly.

"I've been reviewing your file. It's impressive."

"Thank you, ma'am." I was glad I was wearing long sleeves because her raspy voice sent a chill through my body, and goose bumps covered my arms.

"You're a new employee, so I'm sure you'll understand why I'll be scrutinizing you."

"Of course."

"Did you see or hear anything suspicious last night?"

"No."

"Did Paige Andrews ever confide in you about her parents' anti-government activity?"

"No."

"Did you ever attempt to gain her confidence?"

I raised my chin. "Yes. When I was looking through student files, I noticed she was new. From the details of her situation, I suspected she might need counsel, so I sought her out and introduced myself. But she didn't want to talk."

"I see. Why didn't you press the matter? Compel her to talk to you? She could've been withholding crucial information."

Compel her? What a nice way to say forcing someone to talk. I scowled and crossed my arms. "She's a teenager. And I'm a stranger. I figured she'd come to me when I gained her trust. Besides, there was nothing in her file that indicated I *needed* to get her to talk or that such a thing was part of my job description. Pressing a matter and forcing people to talk might work for government officials like you, but those of us who actually care about people realize walking away and giving them space is often the best choice."

Abelard coughed, and Martina's eyes narrowed. "I see," she said. "What other things have you walked away from, Ms. Lloyd?"

More than she realized. "What're you talking about?"

"Was my question unclear?"

"No. Actually, I'd call it obtuse, because I fail to see how your opinion about my handling of Paige Andrews will bring her back. I've worked here for about a week. If there were problems, Paige had them before I got here, and implying that I've done something wrong is rude and inappropriate. I don't like the insinuation that I've not done my job."

Abelard gasped and leaned forward. "Officer Ward, I'm very sorry. Obviously, I need to speak with Ms. Lloyd about conducting herself properly in front of government officials. Please know I had no idea that she—"

Martina glared at Abelard. "Shut up."

He sat back in his chair and shot me a look that was a blend of disbelief and disapproval. I hated myself for letting Martina bother me. Why couldn't I have played it cool and acted subdued? What better way to mark myself as a rebel than fearlessly standing up to someone in the government.

Martina stared at me for a few seconds before shaking her head. "Perhaps your strategy is right. After all, teenagers, and even childish adults, sometimes need to be left alone." A smile spread slowly over her face. "Ms. Lloyd, you're free to go. For now."

I stood. "Thank you."

"It's imperative for you to monitor the girls in your dorm closely. If any of them display attitudes inconsistent with our society's expectations, then you must report them immediately. Walking away in such a case wouldn't be acceptable."

"I understand. And so we're clear, I never walk away from an important fight. I'm in this job for the long haul."

Martina smiled, but it didn't reach her eyes. "With the passion you've displayed, I don't doubt it."

CHAPTER 17

"My dear, what did you say to Martina? According to workplace gossip, you've caused quite a stir." Drake, disguised as Jean, had been spending a lot of time at the academy doing polygraph tests.

Two days after my interview, Drake, Agatha, and I gathered in the safe house living room where I recapped my conversation with Martina.

"She backed down that easily?" Agatha asked. "Doesn't that bother you?"

It did, but I'd already decided if I didn't think about it, the problem might go away. It was probably a dumb strategy, but stewing wasn't going to change what I'd done. I looked at Drake. "How bad is the damage?"

"I never said there was damage. Abelard has gotten over being angry and seems genuinely awed. I offered to do another poly on you, but he said it wasn't necessary. You impressed Martina with your spunk. And your resume. She's fascinated that you speak Spanish and Mandarin. Maybe you're a decent actress after all."

I threw a flowered pillow from the couch at Drake. "Not funny."

He shoved the pillow away, and it fell to the floor, reminding me things weren't right between us.

"We need to talk about how we're going to get two dorms full of students out of government control," he said.

"I talked to our contacts this morning," Agatha said. "They can have a jet ready for us in twenty-four hours if we give them notice."

I pulled the circus flyer from my pocket and handed it to her.

She skimmed it before glancing up, her brow furrowed. "You want to go to the *circus*?"

"Yes. We need to plan a field trip to the circus. A school-wide trip."

Understanding dawned on her face, and she looked at Drake. "What do you think?"

"It's time to get the jet on standby."

* * *

"Don't you think it would be good for the kids to get out and have a fun activity?" I asked Abelard. "It's free. We want the kids to like being here, right? Plus, since the government's sponsoring it, we'll be showing our support and patriotism."

Abelard studied the flyer. "The boys should go too?"

"Definitely." I smiled but stopped short of batting my eyes. There was no need to lay it on too thick.

Abelard cleared his throat. "You like to shake things up, that's for sure. I thought we were both going to be fired when you stood up to Officer Ward like that. You almost gave me diarrhea."

I cringed. I didn't need to know that.

"I've had bowel problems since I was a kid, and anytime I get a shock like that, it's bad news for me."

And the toilet. I had to get this man back on track before he shared any more disgusting information. "So, you're approving the trip? We can go ahead and plan?"

"Yes. I'll let Jake know." Abelard beamed. "Thanks for thinking of this. Our students need something positive after the difficult events this week."

* * *

I dinged my water glass with my fork. The cafeteria quieted, and fifty girls faced my podium. "Before I dismiss you from dinner tonight, I have an announcement. This Saturday, we have tickets for all of you to see the traveling circus that's coming to town."

The long tables of girls aged ten and under buzzed. Emma's face lit up. I caught a few eye rolls from high school girls who exchanged glances. The middle school girls appeared unsure of how to act.

"According to school policy, everyone in preschool, elementary school, and middle school will be required to attend this field trip. High school students are exempt, but we'd love it if you helped chaperone the younger students."

A few high school girls started whispering.

"If you'd like to be a chaperone, please let me know as soon as possible. Ladies, you're dismissed." Chairs scraped the floor, and the girls filed out. A group of high school girls lingered and formed a huddle.

Jake had informed me of the school's field trip policy exempting older students when we'd met to plan. It was my idea to convince the high school students to help us. If they didn't, they were going to be left behind. Most of them would be free in a year or two anyway. Besides, the teenagers could be a liability if they were loyal to the government.

Although, Agatha had assured me it was unlikely the teenagers were. Growing up in a reeducation center usually had the opposite effect of what the government intended. Most of the kids she'd gone to school with were either apathetic or had expressed a desire to help the Emancipation Warriors.

Lilly led the huddle of girls toward me. "Ms. Lloyd? We'd like to help with the kids."

I smiled. It was weird hearing girls my age address me as Ms. Lloyd. "Great. Thank you. I'm sure the younger girls will love it since they look up to you."

"The guys are coming, right?" Lilly asked.

I winked. "Absolutely."

* * *

Saturday arrived, and the stress of planning Operation Circus weighed on my chest as heavily as a herd of performing elephants.

Our scheme had to work.

After an early dinner, we loaded the students on two separate busses. One for boys and one for girls. All but three high school students had agreed to go.

Drake and Agatha wore new disguises and controlled the busses. Even though it was Agatha in disguise, she looked so much older and grandmotherly that I had to stare into her eyes for a few seconds before I believed it was her. Her hands even had liver spots.

It was getting dark when we ushered the students into the coliseum. We had our own line for security, and after scanners confirmed each student's identity, the security team allowed us to take our seats. They'd reserved a block of benches for us in the center of the arena and placed a complimentary box of popcorn at each place.

The students sat down and dug into their popcorn boxes. The high school girls and boys helped the littlest students, and some of them pointed to the three rings on the arena floor. I surveyed a group of four-year-olds. "Everybody okay?"

Emma swallowed a bite of popcorn. "I'm thirsty. Can I have a drink?"

I smiled. "Sure." Looking around, I caught an usher's eye and waved.

A man dressed in red pants and matching red-striped vest came over. "How may I be of service, ma'am?"

"What would it cost to get beverages for these students?" I asked.

He smiled. "For the students of Atlantic Academy? Nothing. I'll get bottles of lemonade and water. Would that be acceptable?"

"Yes, thank you." That was easy.

While the coliseum continued to fill with people, the usher distributed drinks, and soon after, the lights dimmed.

The Jumbotron lit up, and President Cleatus Fortune's reptilian face overtook the screen. The audience cheered, and the students around me stood and clapped.

Seriously? He wasn't actually in the building. But I rose with them.

"Good evening, ladies and gentlemen, boys and girls." He paused and smiled. "It's my pleasure to welcome you to the first annual amateur circus sponsored by the National Academy for the Performing Arts." He drew out the *s*, and the sibilance reminded me of a snake. "All of the performers you will see tonight are students at our prestigious national academy. Due to the war we are fighting, and winning, the instructors felt it would benefit national morale to organize a free traveling circus to delight children and adults in every region."

It was funny what he thought would boost morale. He was like a father tossing a cheap plastic kids' meal toy to his son when what the child wanted was a bike. The idea that liberty could boost morale wasn't even a part of Fortune's worldview.

"We sincerely hope you enjoy the show. Allow me to assure you, this horrible conflict, brought about by rebels who shun peace, will soon be over. We've made significant inroads in the last several months and have destroyed a vast part of their network. In light of that, sit back, relax, and enjoy tonight's performance by some of the best and brightest students in our nation."

Fortune's image on the Jumbotron faded, and organ music resonated. A single spotlight shone on the ringmaster in the center ring. He tipped his hat and began to speak. "This evening, you'll see a show unlike any you've seen before. Tonight, you'll witness an epic battle."

Epic battle? At the circus?

The spotlight faded, and red up-lighting replaced it. The ringmaster continued. "Many years ago, there was a traveling circus."

A holographic tent appeared in the center ring. Performers filed in, and the tent disappeared. Two women and two men wore sparkling blue leotards. Three juggling clowns scuttled around them.

"But the livelihood of the circus was threatened when a group that didn't believe in fun threatened to shut the circus down. We'll call them the Enemies."

Three people dressed in black dropped from the ceiling and crouched menacingly in front of the circus cast. They sprang forward, and the cast formed two huddles. The women screeched. The audience gasped.

I glanced at the younger children who were transfixed on the action in front of them.

The Enemies stood and circled the cast.

"But the performers fought back," the ringmaster said. The performers pulled out swords and made a wall. "They stood firm and battled to keep fun alive. This is the story of their war with the Enemies."

* * *

When we were exiting the coliseum, Fredrica's MD3 buzzed with a coded message from Agatha.

`Your aunt's surgery went well.`

The busses were set. And the jet was ready and waiting.

CHAPTER 18

The bus door closed. My stomach churned, and I prayed our plan would work. In the darkness, students bantered and giggled.

I opened my purse, put my hand inside, and clutched the gas mask. Any second, Agatha would give the signal. We crossed over the bridge spanning the river that ran through town. Agatha glanced in the giant rearview mirror, and we locked eyes. She blinked twice.

I took a deep breath and held.

She reached over and turned the fans on full blast. Children's heads began to droop one by one as the gas permeated the bus.

My chest ached.

When the last student was unconscious, I slipped on my gas mask. Agatha did the same. I knelt next to her, disabled the system that controlled the bus, and tweaked the navigation to show we were on course.

When Agatha took manual control, she drove for another ten minutes, and I paced the aisle monitoring the students. The gas was harmless, and the chemical an agent had put on the popcorn intensified its effect. These kids would be asleep for hours.

Agatha parked the bus in a hangar at an airfield, and Drake pulled in behind us. A large jet waited along with Liam and five other men who wore gas masks. As soon as the busses stopped near the jet, three of the men rushed to our bus. Two came in the front, and each of them immediately grabbed a child, exited the bus, and headed for the plane.

The third man opened the door in the back and hopped on. It was Judd, Emma and Jesse's father. He wore a cowboy hat, and he strode up to me. A look of uncertainty lingered in his expression as he studied my—Fredrica's—face.

"Is that you, Sarah?" He called me by my first alias.

"Yes." I clutched a seatback.

"Drake told me you'd be here and described you, or I wouldn't have recognized you..."

"I'm so sorry. It's my fault Monica—"

"No. You didn't pull the trigger."

"I know, but—"

"But God allowed it because it was her time." He glanced over my shoulder, and his eyes rested on Emma. Brushing past me, he walked to Emma and gathered her in his arms. For a moment, he stood with his face buried in her hair.

Tears sprang to my eyes, and my nose tingled. I'd been Emma's age when my father had died in a car accident. I tried to remember what it'd felt like to have his arms around me.

I couldn't.

Judd lifted his head and met my eyes. "Thank you," he whispered, and he rushed from the bus with Emma.

Gathering another little girl in my arms, I hurried off the bus and up the flight of stairs onto the jet. I buckled her into her seat.

When I exited the plane, Drake was walking toward it with Jesse. Judd intercepted them, took his son in his arms, and wept.

My throat thickened. Would I see *my* son again? Would he ever know how much I loved him? Would I always feel like a piece of my heart was missing?

I took a deep breath, walked back toward the bus, and refocused on our mission. By the time I'd loaded six children, my arms ached.

I glanced at my watch. We needed to hurry. Even though I'd tweaked the navigation system, school security would miss the busses soon. I boarded the bus and grabbed the last girl, who was about eight years old and almost too heavy for me to carry. Only the two Atlantic Academy staff members remained on the bus.

I staggered down the steps, and Drake strode over to take the little girl. I followed him onto the plane and sat in an empty seat.

Drake secured the little girl's seatbelt. "Wait."

"What? She's the last student."

"I know."

"Then we need to get out of here." Agatha was already buckled in, and so were the other men who'd helped.

"You're not going."

"Excuse me?" I got out of my seat and faced Drake in the aisle. "I can't stay behind. The circus was my idea. They'll know I had something to do with it."

"Not necessarily. I'm leaving. We think blame will fall on Jean."

"You *think*. This is my life we're talking about."

"And by standing here arguing with me, you're putting the lives of all these kids in danger. I need you to get off the plane and help Liam get the busses back to the discovery point. You'll be there when the rest of the staff members wake up. They'll never know."

I started to move down the aisle, and Drake followed. "I know you're mad at me," I said, "but why're you changing this at the last minute? You're not even my supervisor anymore." I trudged down the steps and stood in the hangar next to the plane.

"My being upset with you has nothing to do with the change in plans."

"It's Jethro, isn't it?"

"Yes. In fact..." He ran his fingers through his hair. "Remember how you impressed Martina?"

"Yes."

"I overheard her asking Abelard to consider letting you go. She intends to recruit you."

My stomach plummeted to the cement floor. "Why?" We started moving toward the busses.

"You speak Mandarin, and you stood up to her. She thinks you're the perfect combination."

"For what?"

"To work on a new government project in Asia. The whole reason Martina showed up to investigate was because Paige's disappearance could've been a threat to the project. They thought Paige and her parents knew something that would jeopardize it."

I considered what Paige had told me. "This has something to do with Fortune making a deal with the Council of World Peacekeepers?"

"Right. Jethro insists we need to let Martina recruit you so you can figure out what Fortune's up to in Asia."

I covered my face with my hands. This couldn't be happening. Why had my mother insisted I become a multi-lingual freak? I dropped my hands. "And you had to pass this info on to Jethro. You couldn't have kept it to yourself?"

Drake's eyes narrowed. "I was doing my job."

"What if she makes the connection to my real identity? What if she knows I speak Mandarin?"

"Your disguise is doing its job." Drake crossed his arms. "And how many people did you go around telling you speak Mandarin? You never bothered to tell me until recently."

Spanish, yes. Lots of kids at my school spoke Spanish. Mandarin? Not so much. "No one." Even Tindra hadn't known, in all the time we'd studied French together. "But what if my mother or Melvin told Martina when they hired her to be my bodyguard?"

"We'll have to hope they didn't."

"I'd like a little more certainty before I put my neck on the line." My mind buzzed with excuses. I wouldn't be able to help Ben or my mother. I glanced back at the plane.

"Certainty? My dear, we're at war. You don't have the luxury of certainty." He sighed. "I know this is hard. But I agree with Jethro. You're a perfect candidate, especially if Martina needs a translator."

"Can't she use her MD3 for that?"

"Sure she could. But human translators are best. And it's an opportunity for us to get close and figure out what Fortune's up to."

"But what about Canton? Can't I come with you to find him? He might know something important that could help us."

"He might, so in spite of the inconvenience, I'll help you take care of your little promise to the Europeans." He glanced at his courier. "Now go."

I took a step toward the bus and then turned back. "What about the fact I'm a terrible actress? You've said so yourself. Jethro had so little faith in my lying ability, he sent you to give my poly."

Drake put both hands on my shoulders and looked me directly in the eyes. My face heated. "It didn't happen like that. One of my jobs for the Warriors is administering polygraph tests to help our people infiltrate the government." He smirked. "Everything doesn't revolve around you. I didn't falsify results. You passed."

"I did?"

"I wouldn't help convince you if I thought you couldn't do this. For us to have someone on the inside could turn the tide. We suffered a major loss at the Warehouse. Besides, Martina's become a powerful force for the president. He trusts her completely." Drake dropped his hands.

I studied a crack in the cement floor. I couldn't do it.

"Tell me, Vivica, what are you fighting for?"

I met Drake's eyes. He wouldn't like my answer. How many times had he told me joining the Warriors couldn't be about helping Ben? But I loved Ben, and I had to help him. Now that we shared the same faith, we had to have a chance to try our relationship again.

But that wasn't all. My mother's face came to mind, and I thought about the fervent prayer I'd whispered when I'd learned of her impending execution. I had to tell her how the exclusivist Christians were right. Jesus was the only way.

And didn't I want my son growing up in a country without the worry of oppression that we faced? Didn't I long for a normal life myself? Drake stared at me and waited for my answer. Yet under the intensity of his gaze, all of my thoughts became too jumbled to articulate.

"The freedom to have a happy ending," I whispered.

He took my hands and squeezed them gently. "Is that enough?"

"What do you mean?"

"What if your happy ending doesn't happen the way you've planned? What if God has a different ending?"

I wasn't ready to think about that. But I had to. I looked away and dropped his hands. "Promise me something."

"What?" he said.

A lump formed in my throat, and I found it difficult to speak. "If I die, will you get Ben out of prison? Tell him about Isaac and the people who adopted him. And if you can't..." I blinked away tears, but a few escaped. "Look after Isaac yourself."

"You're not going to die on this assignment. That's not what I—"

"You can't guarantee that. Look me in the eyes," I said, meeting his gaze again. "And promise me."

He hesitated. "I promise. Now get out of here or this whole thing is blown."

I threw my arms around him, and he froze. "Thank you."

Chapter 19

"Fredrica. Fredrica. Wake up. You've got to wake up. Something's happened to the students!"

I opened my eyes, and Abelard's splotchy face was inches from my own. I jerked backward and thumped my head against the bus window. "Ow!"

"Oh, be careful, we don't have time for an injury. The police are on the way."

I blinked a few times to allow my eyes to adjust to the morning sunlight and brisk wind that streamed through the open windows.

"What happened?"

"I don't know. I woke up on the other bus, and it was just Jake, Don, and me. No driver. I came over here, and it's just you and the other girls passed out. No driver. No students." Abelard's eyes darted wildly, and he pointed to the windows. "Obviously, they used something to knock us out, so I opened the windows. Jake and Don are still asleep. Who could've done this? And why? Some of the kids are so young. They need us." He put his hands on his head and grasped handfuls of hair. "They can't fend for themselves. And of course there'll be a government investigation. We'll all lose our jobs. Maybe go to prison. Oh, I can't go to prison!"

Abelard continued talking, and I took a few deep breaths and looked at the back of the bus. Two teachers, Orchid and Earlene, slumped in their seats. I stood but was dizzy and clutched the seat back in front of me.

"Who would do this?" Abelard stared at me as though he wanted an answer, but I wasn't sure why he was depending on me to give it to him.

I yawned. "Could a rebel group do something like this?"

"You think we've been infiltrated? It had to be someone on the inside. Someone who knew we were going to the circus."

I rubbed the back of my neck. I'd fallen asleep in a strange position. "Maybe. It could've been someone at the circus too. The organizers knew we were coming. They reserved seats. Provided the transportation…" I moved out of my seat, walked down the aisle, and stopped at Earlene's seat. I tapped her on the shoulder, figuring she'd appreciate a gentle wake-up call rather than opening her eyes to Abelard's frantic face.

Sirens wailed in the distance.

Earlene moaned and opened her eyes. "Where am I?"

I gave her a few details and moved on to Orchid before Abelard could. When he saw I was taking care of the women, he darted off the bus and posted himself next to the road until the police arrived.

* * *

It was late afternoon when I arrived back at the dorm. I'd given my statement to the police and dodged an onslaught of reporters. I'd probably said the words, "No comment," at least twenty times.

I tapped in the security code for my courier and discovered a voice message from Agatha. "The students are all safe. There was a lot of commotion when they woke up. The little ones were scared, and the older ones were excited. We probably have some new recruits from this bunch. Anyway, we're putting them in good foster homes in remote locations and giving them new IDs. I'll keep you posted."

I flopped onto the couch. There were a lot of things I should do, but I didn't have the energy for any of them. I needed to pray, but I couldn't find the words.

My thoughts were interrupted by someone rapping on my door. I stuffed my courier under the couch cushion. "Coming!" I peered through the peephole and stifled a groan.

Martina.

I opened the door. "How may I help you, ma'am?"

"Good evening, Ms. Lloyd. I need to speak with you." She brushed me aside and walked in with a slight limp from a gunshot wound.

"Please. Have a seat. Would you like something to drink?"

"No." She commandeered a chair. "I've read your statement on the police report. You have a better grasp than anyone that this act could be the work of the rebels."

I shrugged and sat on the couch. "Who else would it be? Anyone who's been paying attention should know that." I wanted to say it could be the work of the government relocating the students to another reeducation center and blaming the rebels, but that would look suspicious.

"Precisely. Yet there are other staff members spinning ridiculous stories such as criminals holding the children hostage for ransom. Too many people in this country don't pay attention. Even in the middle of a war. That's why I need your help."

I raised my eyebrows. "My help?"

"I've already spoken to Abelard about this, but since most of the students are gone, his previous concerns are irrelevant. Come work for me."

I feigned surprise. "Why? I'm just a teacher with a background in psychology."

Martina smiled. "You're young. Smart. Multilingual. And you're not easily intimidated. That's the kind of person I want on my team. I used to work in Population Management, and after that, private security. I'm currently working on a special project for the president."

"Yet you took time out to come here and investigate a school?"

"Yes, I did. And with good reason."

I toyed with the idea of making her mad enough to forget about recruiting me, but the memory of Drake's plea stopped me. "I understand you have to be discreet. What would I be doing?"

"You'd evaluate citizens' skills to determine the best roles for them in a new project." Her eyes gleamed. "There's international travel. It'd be more interesting than being stuck in this school."

"It sounds cool." I forced myself to sound enthusiastic and prayed it didn't sound fake.

She eyed me. "I sense some hesitation. I'm a powerful woman, and I can make your career with this move. I take orders directly from President Fortune, and I'm one of his trusted advisors."

"Yes ma'am."

"Can I count you as a part of my team?"

"Definitely."

"Excellent. Now, you'll have a biochip implanted in your arm. Soon, the Council of World Peacekeepers will require it of everyone, but government officials are first. After that, we'll travel home to Union City."

"Awesome."

I remembered how smug my mother had been when she'd first told me about the biochips that would monitor everyone's health. But they'd also make it easier for the government to track citizens.

* * *

I waited on a bed in the infirmary basement the next morning and swung my legs back and forth. Dr. Pervert wrenched the door open.

My legs slowed, and my fingers dug into the edge of the cot.

"I'm Dr. Calgary. I'll be inserting your biochip."

He'd always be Dr. Pervert to me. "Great. I'm pumped to work for Officer Ward."

He opened a pouch and removed a wipe. "Push up your sleeve on your right arm."

I did, and he cleaned my upper arm. Then he fished his ID from his pocket, swiped a keypad on a cabinet, and unlatched the door. He withdrew a retinal scanner. "Hold still, and don't blink."

"What's this for?"

"Syncs your chip with your retinas." He studied the scanner's display and pushed a few buttons. Then he grabbed a plastic device with a thick needle and scanned it.

I chewed the inside of my cheek. "Umm…are you going to numb my arm before you jab that monster needle in?"

He scowled, stalked to another cabinet, took out some medicine and injected my upper arm. I winced. "What happens if that chip moves out of place?"

"It won't. The outer coating knits with your muscle after about twenty-four hours."

I cringed.

"Is your arm numb yet?"

"Yep."

He jabbed the needle into my arm and inserted the chip. After he extracted the needle, he covered the wound with a bandage. "You're free to go."

* * *

Two days later, in my new Union City apartment, I grimaced as I donned my government-issued uniform. Not only did my right arm ache from the insertion of the biochip, but I had to wear an ugly uniform. The blue button-down shirt was to be starched to perfection. The pants were black and fit too high on the waist to be considered either youthful or fashionable. I wound my hair into a tight bun at the nape of my neck and hoped my appearance would meet Martina's standards. Actually, I didn't care about her approval.

But Fredrica did.

I'd be present for the first part of the meeting with President Fortune, after which I'd be dismissed while she stayed and received classified information.

It was a perfect opportunity to plant the bug Jethro had given me in the office.

In order to bypass security, I'd have to smuggle in the device in two parts. The first fit under the stone on a ring. The second fit into my pocket. After a few hours, it would deactivate, so it wouldn't be detected in a security sweep. I grabbed Fredrica's MD3 and hid my courier under the carpet in my closet.

I arrived in the lobby early and lounged on a leather couch while I waited for Martina. The walls were a stark eggshell color, and the art on the walls contained abstract shapes in various shades of red.

The elevator dinged and Martina exited. I jumped up. Duff, the thug Martina had hired to replace Axel, trailed behind. She looked me up and down a few times before nodding. "Let's go. Lateness is rude, especially when meeting with an important man like the president."

As Martina and I settled in the back seat of the blue sedan, I wondered if she was going to take advantage of every moment to teach me a lesson.

"How was your day off?" I asked.

"Fine." Martina lowered her MD3 to her lap, and I caught a glimpse of a little girl's picture.

"Is that your daughter?" I pointed at the device.

"Asking personal questions to your superiors is neither necessary nor appropriate." She turned the MD3 face down.

Another lesson.

I stared out the window and studied the Union City scenery. The last time I'd been to the capital, Fortune had been vice-president, and I'd watched the assassination of President Hernandez—while he was announcing my mother would replace him at the end of his term. My mother narrowly escaped being killed, and my bodyguard had taken the bullet meant for her.

Since the presidential mansion was located outside of Union City for security reasons, and to give the president a retreat, he kept an office within the city limits. That's where we headed.

The building was located a block from the capitol building, where the legislative body had met until the building had been destroyed several months ago. The government blamed the rebels, but I suspected they destroyed their own building into order to create a reason to go to war. The government had to sway public opinion somehow.

The president's office was made of limestone, and the first floor had been fitted with stained glass windows that contained a picture representing each of the seven regions. The windows on the other floors displayed designs from artists around the country. Red, one of the national colors, was used heavily.

The whole effect reminded me of pictures of churches from long ago, which wasn't surprising. Many in this country revered the president as if he were a god.

Security included a pat down and a full-body scan. Then, there was the usual retinal scan. I hoped whatever had been done to my eyes was still effective. I held my breath until the scanner gave a friendly beep and a guard waved me forward. Another guard confiscated my MD3, as I'd expected.

I followed Martina and Duff down a marble hall. Mahogany double doors beckoned at the end of the hallway. When we were a few feet away, the doors opened, and we stepped onto plush, royal blue carpet.

"Welcome to the office of the president," a familiar voice said.

My stomach lurched when I met the eyes of Melvin Powers—my mother's former assistant.

CHAPTER 20

When I'd learned of my mother's arrest, my first instinct had been to suspect Melvin. His new position confirmed what I'd thought.

He'd turned her in to save himself.

A slight man with graying hair, Melvin was past age fifty and had missed his own chance to become a politician, so he made a living being a toady for those in power. He'd bet on my mother and lost. Now he'd picked another losing candidate, even if he didn't know it yet. He was no doubt enjoying being this close to influence while it lasted.

Knowing he'd abandoned my mother in favor of the man who'd tried to assassinate her made my chest tight. Yet, I couldn't afford to look furious, so I gave Melvin a polite smile and curt nod.

"Melvin, this is Fredrica Lloyd. I'm training her," Martina said.

He extended his hand. "It's a pleasure to meet you. I'm Melvin Powers."

I shook his callous-free hand. "Nice to meet you." I hoped the words didn't seem as forced as they felt.

Why had I once thought of this man as a father figure?

"If you will please follow me to the boardroom, the president will arrive shortly," Melvin said.

Cream-colored wallpaper with vertical pale gold stripes decorated the hall. The effect was regal, and portraits of former presidents lined the walls. When we passed President Hernandez's portrait, a chill passed over my body, and I recalled the day he'd died.

Though his misguided policies had helped oppress our country, he'd been a nice man who'd loved his family. He'd always had a kind word for me when I'd accompanied my mother on state visits to Union City.

The boardroom had the same paper as the hall, and an oval table sat in the middle. My mother's former head of security, Director Spiegel, waited. So he'd leveraged a promotion too. That wasn't surprising. His thoughts about controlling the Emancipation Warriors through executions were more in line with Fortune's ideals than my mother's. Spiegel was in his fifties and popped antacids like candy.

Martina introduced me to Director Spiegel, and I clasped his hand before I took a seat next to her at the table. Duff stood outside the door. While she made small talk with Director Spiegel, I slipped my right hand into my pocket and turned my ring around toward my thumb. The top part of the ring looked like a stone, but it was a cap that concealed half of the bug in a hollow. When the piece came out, I flipped the cap back on the ring and fished for the other piece in my pocket.

Piecing them together with one hand and without being able to see them was difficult. I kept my eyes on Martina and the men. I needed to look like I was paying attention. Every so often, I nodded when the others did.

Fortune entered the room. I had to get the pieces snapped together soon because I didn't know how long I'd be a part of this meeting. Martina and the director rose, so I had to do the same. While the president went to Director Spiegel and shook his hand, I fought with the pieces. With every second that passed, my fingers lost dexterity.

When I thought I had the pieces fitted, they slipped apart. The president greeted Martina with a kiss on the cheek.

"How was your weekend?" she asked.

Did she not know it was neither necessary nor appropriate to ask a personal question of her superior? The edge of my mouth quivered, and I glanced away.

Just as Fortune answered, I snapped the bug's pieces together. He faced me, and I shoved the device into my pocket.

"You must be Fredrica," Fortune said, extending his hand. My hand disappeared inside his dry one, and he clasped his other hand over mine, entrapping it. "It's a pleasure to meet you. You'll be able to learn so much from Martina. As you may know, I was once a professor, and she was one of my brightest students."

"I'm sure she was."

"I'm delighted she's come back to work for me." He moved away and took his seat at the head of the table. "Martina, will you give a report on your investigation at Atlantic Academy?"

"Yes. My original investigation centered on the disappearance of a young girl named Paige Andrews." Martina's gaze flicked in my direction. "Paige was of particular interest to us because after her escape, we feared she might spread information about our special project that she'd learned from her parents, who've now been executed. Since this project cannot be made public, it was crucial that we neutralize the threat."

"Which we've still been unable to do." Fortune scowled. "Now the problem is worse."

Martina clasped her hands. "We've believe the person involved in helping Paige escape is the same person who's responsible for the mass kidnapping. His name is Jean Leblanc."

Fortune squinted. "An alias?"

"I'm sure." Martina sighed. "Every one of the employees passed background checks and polygraphs. Not a single person has rebel ties, but since Leblanc was the one who disappeared after the kidnapping, we believe he was the only one involved. He's worked all over the country administering polygraphs for the government. His references were impeccable."

"Bottom line," Fortune said. "Somehow the rebels infiltrated on Geissler's watch. And the kidnapping on yours. How damaging is this to our project?"

Martina blanched. "I see no reason not to continue, though we may want to speed up our timeline. Which is why I've brought Ms. Lloyd on board. She'll be helpful in assessing and assigning citizens."

Assessing and assigning citizens to what? When was I going to get clarification? I slipped the bug out of my pocket and wedged it into the crack between the upholstery and wood on my chair.

Fortune steepled his fingers. "Director Spiegel, send the police to arrest Abelard Geissler. Someone has to be held accountable. And I want every place that Leblanc gave polygraphs scrutinized. He could've placed rebels all over the country."

"Yes sir. I'll make the calls now." He rushed out.

"Now would be a good time to dismiss Ms. Lloyd," Martina said. "The remaining items on our agenda are classified."

"I agree," President Fortune said.

I stood. "Thank you for this wonderful opportunity. It was lovely meeting all of you gentlemen."

When I walked out, Melvin waited for me at the end of the hallway. He pointed to a seating area across from a wooden desk that I hadn't noticed when we'd entered the president's offices earlier. I chose a couch with an ornate blue, red, and gold print.

"May I offer you something to drink?" he asked.

"Water would be nice, please."

I almost went to snoop at his desk, but I thought better of it when my casual glance at the ceiling revealed four security cameras.

Melvin returned with a bottle of water. "Here you go, sweetie." He studied me for a moment, and my heart started to race.

"You remind me of someone I used to know," he said.

"Really?" I removed the cap from the bottle.

"You look nothing like her. Well, you're tall like she is. But that's not it. Lots of young ladies are tall. It's the presence you have when you enter a room."

My grip on the water bottle increased, causing a faint, plastic snap. What if Martina had noticed the same thing? "You said you *used* to know her. What happened?"

Melvin sat on the arm of the couch and studied his hands. "It was a tragic situation. She was the daughter of a woman I worked for. The poor girl got in with the wrong crowd and ended up disappearing."

"When you say wrong crowd, do you mean the rebels?" I sipped water and prayed I appeared casual.

"Yes, I believe that's what happened." He brushed some dog hair from his pant leg.

I scowled. "The rebels killed my sister. It sickens me every time I hear of someone taking their side. They have to pay for what they've done to destroy our country."

Melvin studied his hands. "I'm sorry to hear about your sister. Is that why you're working with Officer Ward?"

"It's why I started working at Atlantic Academy. Officer Ward took me from the staff when she was there investigating."

"I see. That was an impressive career change." There was no mistaking the skepticism and question in his voice. *Why would Officer Ward pick a lowly staff member from a reeducation center?* But I couldn't give him the reason. Melvin knew Vivica spoke Mandarin.

I sat straighter and smiled. "Yes. It was. I'm very lucky."

Melvin glanced toward the boardroom door then fastened his gaze back on me. "If I may be so bold, may I offer you advice?"

I crossed my arms. "What's that?"

"Learn everything you can from Officer Ward. But never let her manipulate you."

"Why do you say that?" I fought laughter. The idea of Melvin offering advice on not allowing someone to manipulate you was ludicrous. My mother had played him for years.

He held up a hand. "Please. I don't mean to insult your superior, but her tactics can be unconventional. Make sure you understand what role you're playing in her grand scheme. I've never known her to voluntarily train anyone." Melvin stood. "Anyway, I only want to caution you. Just because you remind me…"

I smiled. "Of course." I relaxed back against the couch and met his eyes. My makeup, the eye color, the change in my voice did nothing to fool him.

He knew I was Vivica Wilkins.

And if he saw past my disguise, then I couldn't be sure about Martina.

CHAPTER 21

After the meeting, I returned to my apartment and retrieved my courier from under the carpet in my closet. I was eager to hear what else had been discussed in the meeting with President Fortune, but I had a message from Drake.

Call me. ASAP.

The meeting would have to wait.

"I'm in town, and I need to see you. Go to your hall closet."

I laughed. "Are you planning to teleport me to your location?"

"Teleporting would make things easier. But, no. Are you at the closet?"

"Yes." I opened the door and was surprised to see a tennis bag, a set of golf clubs, a soccer ball, football, and basketball.

"There a tennis racket?"

I knelt down and unzipped the bag. It had two rackets, and there were three unopened containers of tennis balls. "Yeah. How'd you know?"

"You're in a government apartment. And our keepers like their workers to stay active. If you check your bedroom closet, there's probably a cute little tennis outfit in your size."

I walked to the bedroom and inspected the back of my closet. The outfit was in a garment bag along with other athletic clothes. Creepy.

"Change clothes. Take the tennis bag with you on the subway. Get off at the Fulton station. Three blocks to the north, there's a building with a set of indoor courts. I'll be there waiting."

* * *

Drake pulled the tab on a container of tennis balls, and it hissed open. He bounced a ball in my direction. "Our lesson today will be on how to serve," he said. He'd changed his disguise from the last time I'd seen him, and now instead of brown, his hair had a strawberry blond tint. His nose was long and straight, his chin was rounder, and his eyes were a dark blue.

I reminded myself that Fredrica was an inept tennis player. "You have your work cut out for you."

The indoor tennis center had five courts. We took court number five, which was farthest from the lobby. Only court number one was occupied, and the two men were in the middle of a close match, at least it appeared that way from the intensity of their volleys. It reminded me of my days when I'd played on the tennis team at my high school. Days that seemed as though they belonged in another lifetime…

Drake gave a demonstration on how to serve and motioned for me to step closer. When I did, he whispered, "Pretend I'm giving you instructions."

I tossed the ball in the air.

"Tell me what you've learned so far."

I swung my racket at the ball and missed. "Shouldn't I be passing that onto Heavyweight?"

"No." Drake stepped forward, caught the ball, and handed it to me.

"Why not?" I attempted a second serve. This time I made contact with the ball, but it died in the net.

"Heavyweight's overloaded. I told him I'd give you a second chance."

I said a silent prayer of thanks for Jethro's busyness. "Admit it. You missed me." I served again, and the ball plopped over the net. I cheered and pumped my fist.

"My dear, that was the wrong side of the court. Toss the ball higher."

I frowned. "You seriously think I don't know that?" I whispered. "You couldn't have called to tell me this?"

"And miss seeing you in a tennis skirt?"

My face burned, and I swatted at him with the racket. "What would Moonbeam say about that?"

He laughed and grabbed the racket from my hand. "Nothing, because my relationship with Moonbeam is purely professional."

But there was something in Drake's tone. "Sure it is. That's why you want to date her. Or are you already dating?"

"I've learned my lesson about dating coworkers."

"Oh, so you've thought about it. I was right."

"I'm not dating Moonbeam."

"I don't believe you. You're protesting too much."

"It doesn't matter if you believe me or not. But since you're goading me, I'm setting you straight."

I grinned. Drake acted this way when someone got too close to the truth. It didn't matter. I'd find out from Agatha.

"Are you going to tell me about the meeting with Fortune or not?" Drake put the racket back in my hand and adjusted the position. "Try that."

I tossed the tennis ball in the air, made contact, and the shot landed perfectly on the correct side of the court. This time, I jumped up and down and cheered. He gave me a high five, and I filled him in on what I'd learned at the meeting, including the fact they were onto his alias.

"I guess my days as a polygraph examiner are over. I was getting tired of it anyway." He glanced over my shoulder and waved. "Your new tennis partner's here."

My eyes widened as a clean-shaven man strode toward us bouncing a tennis ball. "Hear you're looking for me." The cynicism in his eyes and voice was familiar, but I didn't recognize the man's face.

I glanced at Drake who nodded.

I couldn't believe how different Canton looked without his beard.

Canton pocketed the tennis ball. "How come the evidence I gave you on Fortune never made it to the press?"

"I gave it to my mother, but that didn't work out. She's in prison now."

"I've heard. Why'd you think it was a good idea to give it to her?"

"It had to come from a credible source if the media was going to accept it. At the time, she was the best choice. It's not my fault someone betrayed her. I believe she intended to use it." I'd thought Melvin had turned in my mother. But since his gentle warning to Fredrica, I wasn't sure.

Canton shook his head. "You have questions for me, then let's get it over with. I'm willing to tell the two of you what I know because there's a chance you can help. It's a long shot, though, since our organization hasn't been listening to me. It's why I disappeared." He glared at Drake. "Still don't know how you found me."

"I'm that good."

Canton scowled.

"Do you have a problem with me recording the conversation for the Europeans?" I asked.

"I don't trust anyone," Canton said. "Especially not foreign intelligence officers, no matter how friendly they seem. But sometimes you got to work with them to achieve a bigger goal. Do what you have to do. But when we're done here, I'm gone."

I turned on my courier's recorder.

"The two of you get over here. Pretend like I'm showing you something funny." Canton held out his courier, and Drake and I bent to look. We both faked laughs.

"All right. Ask away." Canton shoved his device in his pocket.

"What do you know about the Peacemaker?"

Canton raised his eyebrows. "So the Europeans suddenly think that's important?"

"It's not?" I asked.

"Could be." He bounced the ball a few times. "When I worked undercover in Pop Management with Martina, I overheard her refer to the Peacemaker a few times while she was talking to the president. But at the time, it didn't seem relevant. The best I could figure, the Peacemaker was a person."

Drake leaned on his racket. "Man or woman?"

"Don't know. But they're working on some kind of special government project. Top secret."

There it was. The special project I didn't have details about. "But you have no idea what that was."

"No, but at the time, Martina said some things that made me suspect the Council of World Peacekeepers may've been involved in funding the whole deal."

"Any idea where we can find this Peacemaker?" Drake asked.

"Asia."

Drake and I exchanged glances.

Canton's eyes lit up. "Let me check something." He took his courier back out of his pocket and scrolled. "Yep. There it is." He pointed to satellite photos of a city with the same latitude and longitude label on the bottom of each picture. "These pics were projected on her wall one day after I heard her talking about the Peacemaker, so I took some shots with my courier when she stepped out. I checked the coordinates. The city's in northern Asia." His fingers flew over his courier. "I'll send you copies."

"But you have no idea why this city is significant?" I asked.

"Nope. Maybe it's where the special project is taking place. Or the Peacemaker lives there." Canton returned his courier to his pocket and spun his racket. "That's all I've got. I came for tennis. So let's play. I'll take on the two of you before I split."

"Good call," Drake said.

* * *

The Peacemaker had to be connected to the special project. But how? As soon as we were done playing tennis, Canton had disappeared, and Drake had left. I sent the recording to Chad and finally had a moment to listen to the rest of Fortune's meeting with Martina and Director Spiegel.

"Give me an update on the Wilkins girl," Fortune said.

"Yes sir," Director Spiegel said. "We've been unable to locate her, though we did manage to shut down another rebel training camp." There was a faint rattle of a wrapper. No doubt he was retrieving an antacid tablet.

"It's ridiculous we haven't been able to find her," Martina said. "That little sneak deserves to die along with her mother."

I shivered.

"I don't think so." Fortune cleared his throat. "Her hacking skills will be as valuable to us as the Peacemaker's."

The Peacemaker was a hacker?

"Keeping her alive isn't worth the risk," Martina said. "She's proven—"

Thwack!

"It's worth it if I say so," Fortune spat.

"Shall we move onto Project Harmony?" Director Spiegel said.

"Yes." There was a hint of relief in Martina's voice. "I spoke with our liaison in Asia this morning, and the city's ready for citizens as soon as we complete the evaluations of our prisoners."

Frowning, I grabbed my courier and scrolled through the pictures from Canton, zooming in on each one. Why hadn't we noticed this before? No cars on the road. No signs of life. The city was empty.

"What about price? Are they ready to negotiate?" Fortune asked.

"Yes. In fact, I'm sending you a list of the suggested prices. Obviously some prisoners will be worth far more than others."

Hadn't one of the soldiers mentioned price during the raid on the Warehouse? The memory of the soldiers' argument over the dead rebels skittered through my mind.

Twenty-seven rebels would've brought a hefty price.

A wave of dizziness rolled through my vision when I finally understood the secret project.

Fortune was selling prisoners to fill the city.

CHAPTER 22

I took a deep breath and concentrated on the rest of the conversation.

"Wonderful," Fortune said. "Now, I'd like to speak to you alone, Martina. Director, you may be excused for a few moments. We'll call you in when we're ready for you again."

A door opened and closed.

"What is it?" Martina asked. I detected apprehension in her tone.

"You may be welcome in my bedroom, but you have no right to undermine me in a meeting. I cannot tolerate that. And I won't."

Ick. That was more information than I wanted to know about Martina and the president.

"I'm sorry. It won't happen again. You know I want what's best for you."

I'd never heard Martina take such a humble approach with anyone. Even her raspy voice had a note of sweetness. Or was it fear?

"See that it never happens again."

* * *

The next morning, Martina folded her hands and rested them on her desk. "I'd like to explain your assignment, but first I need to acquaint you with our special project." She stood and swiped her hand across the screen behind her. A picture of a city skyline appeared, along with the words *Project Harmony* written in red. "President Fortune gave me permission to read you in, because he believes you'll be a valuable member of our team."

"Thank you for your faith in me."

"As you're aware, we're at war. Unfortunately, that conflict is costing our nation respect with the Council of World Peacekeepers. They're threatening a complete takeover of the country unless we get the rebels under control."

Since Fortune was a Globalist, I wondered why the Peacekeepers taking over would be negative. But to stay in power and appease the Nationalists, the illusion of maintaining national sovereignty was probably important. "And this project will help?"

Martina smiled. "Of course. We must get rid of the people who are disturbing the peace and who disagree with the principles that are necessary for maintaining order. Killing them is one option, but there's a better choice. That's where Project Harmony comes in. What you see on the screen is an empty city in the Republic of Asia." She brushed her hand across the screen, and a satellite map appeared. "This city is in a remote location and has everything necessary to be self-sustaining. Apartments, office buildings, hospitals, and schools. The Asians built it many years ago, but they've not been able to populate it due to its location, so they sold it to the Council of World Peacekeepers. We've made a secret deal with the Peacekeepers to fill it with rebels in exchange for financial help. Well, rebels who meet the city's needs."

I forced myself to focus. "What exactly is the city for?"

Martina smiled. "It's a prototype for the kind of city the Peacekeepers hope to build around the world in the future, in order to bring about world peace and harmony. Right now, it's experimental. Some of the wealthiest people in the world have invested in this city." She chuckled. "It's like a game to them."

"How so?"

"You'll see when you get there." She waved a hand.

I hated that answer because I needed all the information I could get. I leaned forward and made sure my eyes gleamed. "What about the rest of the prisoners?"

"Execution. But killing them all is wasteful when the Peacekeepers are willing to pay a high price for qualified citizens. Cleatus believes the money can be used to help with economic recovery."

I ignored my churning stomach. I was Fredrica. And she hated rebels. "Perfect. How will I be able to help?"

"I'm leaving for Asia soon. You're coming with me to translate, since there are some Mandarin-speaking employees who work for the Peacekeepers. But first, you're going to assess prisoners at Union City Federal Detention Center, so we can decide who'll be making the trip with us."

"You mean I get to decide if they'll be a slave or die?" I had to make sure I assessed Ben and my mother.

"You sound so eager." She emitted a throaty chuckle. "But, yes, that's right."

I sat back in my chair and crossed my arms. "How many slaves do we need?"

"Don't use the term *slaves.* Call them *citizens.*" Her forehead wrinkled. "The city can hold millions. However, we're filling it slowly with prisoners from all over the country. The accommodations are an upgrade from prison." She changed the screen, and a picture of a small apartment appeared. "This is a standard issue apartment. Six hundred square feet. One bedroom. Perfect for singles." She swiped the screen. "However, we recognize that the city must be self-sustaining in the future, so families are necessary. This is a three-bedroom apartment that'll be issued to families with children."

"I see." Would entire families make the trip?

"Obviously, families are not our first concern. We'll populate the city with essential personnel first. We can always create families if necessary." She leaned back in her chair. "In fact, desirable genetic traits are part of our selection process."

One more way to control people. A chill skittered down my spine.

"I've sent a document to your MD3 that'll help you assess the prisoners at Union City prison. It'll tell you what questions to ask, what qualities to look for, and how to determine the subject's usefulness to our project."

I took a deep breath, smiled, and knocked back encroaching horror. "I'm so glad you've trusted me with such an important assignment." I stood. "I'll start reading right away."

"Be at the prison tomorrow morning at eight."

Clutching Fredrica's MD3, I left the office. How could I play with the lives of my fellow citizens?

And Christians.

CHAPTER 23

I paced the living room floor in the safe house while Drake lounged in a recliner. "This is your fault." I stopped and pointed at him. "You got me into this. If you hadn't forced me to go with Martina—"

"Let's back up and review our history. The night we met at the governor's ball, you'd already managed to get yourself into the trouble that eventually led you here. So, my dear, I suggest you turn your pretty little finger around."

I dropped my hand. "Do you understand what Martina wants me to do? Do you comprehend the choices I'm going to be forced to make?"

Drake's expression softened. "I do. And we should talk about that."

"What do you mean?"

"Ben. Your mother."

"Right. I need to make sure they meet the government's criteria." I resumed pacing.

"I was afraid you'd say that."

I whirled around. "What're you trying to say?"

"You have to evaluate them like everyone else."

"I can't. We're talking about people I love."

Drake leaned forward and rested his head in his hands. The silence ballooned between us. Why was he just sitting there? Finally, he looked up. I'd never seen such compassion in his expression before. He stood and guided me to the couch.

"I know you love them. If I were in your position, I'm not sure I could objectively evaluate the people I love. But we're approaching this the wrong way."

"Why?"

"I'm not good at talking about spiritual stuff, but I'm trying to do better." He blew out a deep breath. "The whole situation with Faith knocked me off my feet and made me realize I need to quit trying to do everything my way instead of God's." He paused. "We're forgetting that God's ultimately in control of every life in that prison. Right now, he's put you in a position to help spare the lives of certain people."

"It's not fair."

The muscle in Drake's jaw twitched. "Seems that way, doesn't it?" He shook his head. "I keep thinking of that verse in Isaiah. 'For my thoughts are not your thoughts, neither are your ways my ways—'"

"That's something I still don't get about God." My throat thickened.

"But God goes on to say that his ways and thoughts are higher than ours."

I wasn't so sure.

"So we're going to have to trust him to take care of the others who don't meet the government's criteria."

"And that might include my mother and Ben."

Drake took my hand and gave it a gentle squeeze.

* * *

Union City Federal Detention Center was a limestone fortress. I pulled my jacket tighter as I braced against the autumn air that howled on this rainy morning. Sodden leaves, once glorious flames on proud trees, plastered the sidewalk leading to the prison entrance. Martina's words yesterday still iced my soul, and reading the prisoner evaluation document had done nothing to thaw bitter truth.

But today I was Fredrica, ruthless and driven by memories of her sister's death. When I'd read the booklet last night after talking to Drake, I'd realized few prisoners would meet the criteria. The booklet's harsh list lingered in my mind.

Criteria for Participation in Project Harmony

1. The citizen must rank in the 85th percentile or above in government intelligence tests.
2. The citizen must be in good health as determined by government physicians and psychiatrists.
3. The citizen must not carry any genes with defects or diseases.
4. The citizen must be above average in appearance.
5. The citizen's weight must not exceed the recommended range for his or her height.

Exceptions to one or more of the following criterion may be made should the government evaluator determine the citizen possesses skills that will benefit Project Harmony. The government is specifically looking for citizens who are skilled in technology and those who can speak multiple languages. However, other skills may be deemed necessary when the needs of the city are established.

Both my mother and Ben were fine as far as health, weight, and appearance. I was fairly certain they'd both fit the intelligence criterion, but either of them could have a genetic flaw that nobody knew about until now. Whatever the results of genetic testing, I had to find a way Ben and my mother could contribute a skill necessary to Project Harmony. I pushed through the prison door, and after a security check, a guard escorted me to a waiting room. A row of metal folding chairs lined the dingy wall. I balanced on the edge, and the chilled metal bit through my thin uniform pants.

"Ms. Lloyd?" A middle-aged black woman stood in the waiting room doorway. Though she was average in build, her bearing and perfect posture commanded my attention. I stood, and she extended her hand and walked toward me.

"I'm Warden Clark. Let's get you to your workspace." She led the way down the hall. "This prison is brimming with rebels. Project Harmony will relieve some of that burden." She stopped and pointed to an open door. The tiny room had a desk, two chairs, and a computer.

"Thank you," I said. Where was I supposed to start? I couldn't appear as though I didn't know what was going on. I walked around the desk and settled in the chair behind the computer.

"You'll find files for each prisoner on the computer. Recently, we've had every rebel prisoner take an intelligence test. Our staff physician and psychiatrist also evaluated them. The results of the genetic tests are in the files along with everything else."

I smiled. "That's very helpful."

She removed bifocals from her head, donned them, stepped around the desk, and stood behind me. "Let me show you how to use this program. Officer Ward said your one weakness is technology."

I laughed, thankful Martina had bought that little lie. "True, but I get by." The prisoners' files were easy to understand and navigate, but I feigned confusion for a minute or two before I pretended to have a breakthrough. The last thing I wanted was for Warden Clark to think I was incompetent.

"Can you handle it from here?"

"Absolutely. The program is user friendly."

She moved toward the door. "Go through each of the files. Use the criteria to make a list of prisoners you'd like to interview. Once you have the list, I'll make arrangements for you."

"Do I have a goal or a limit?"

She removed her glasses and shrugged. "No. Do whatever you think is best for the project. We'll dispose of the rest." Her face brightened. "Would you like something to drink?"

I started to say no, but my tongue stuck to the roof of my mouth. "Water, please."

* * *

Knowing the government likely monitored all activity on the computer, I resisted the urge to go directly to Ben's and my mother's files. I even had to assume security cameras watched this room, so demonstrating emotion was forbidden.

I was Fredrica.

God, please help me.

I sipped the water Warden Clark had delivered and evaluated the files in alphabetical order. The first three prisoners didn't make the list because they didn't meet the intelligence or health criteria. Combing each of their files for skills that would save them, I found no way to justify putting them on the interview list.

A lump formed in my throat and tears pricked my eyes, but I recalled Drake's advice. *God, I don't like making the decision about these people. Please save them. Provide another way.*

When I finished my prayer, I moved on. Because I had to.

CHAPTER 24

I'd finished evaluating prisoners whose last names started with the letter *K* and was ready to move to *L* when Warden Clark threw open the office door. A rush of cool air blasted my face. "Lunch time," she said. "We don't want to be late for our reservation."

My stomach burned. "I'd be happy to stay here and work through lunch since this is important."

Warden Clark waved a hand. "Nonsense. President Fortune is buying lunch, and I'm not missing an opportunity to eat at one of the best restaurants in Union City because you have a hankering to work through lunch. Officer Ward insisted I bring you. So, chop chop."

"Of course. I *am* hungry." Ben's file would have to wait.

I followed the warden outside to an executive car from President Fortune's fleet. The sun remained hidden behind heavy clouds, and a fine drizzle dampened the air. The uniformed guard opened the doors for us and programmed the car. When we were on our way, Warden Clark turned to me. "How many do you have on the list?"

"Of 143 prisoners, I've found 22 who meet the criteria. Quite a few have genetic predispositions to certain diseases, but given their skill sets, I don't think it's worth disposing of them based on illnesses that might develop or be curable by the time they do." I hated using the word *dispose,* but Fredrica would.

"Yes, I tend to agree with you. I'm impressed with your efficiency."

"Thank you."

"Have you had to eliminate anyone 'cause they're ugly?" Her eyes danced.

My heart flipped, and I blinked a few times. "Nah. Lack of intelligence gets most people."

"Dumb and ugly go together?"

I forced a laugh. "It sure seems that way."

The driver took us to an exclusive district in Union City, known for its fine dining and shopping. In spite of the dismal weather, women wearing fashionable raincoats and toting bulging shopping bags paraded past clothing boutiques.

I used to be like them.

The driver pulled to the curb next to Antonio's, a fine-dining restaurant. When we entered, the restaurant's lunchtime crowd buzzed. Silverware clinked against china. The host led us past tables laden with high-quality linens and down a short hallway, where he opened a carved oak door, revealing a private dining room. Martina waited at a round table with President Fortune, Director Spiegel, Melvin, and a white-haired man I didn't recognize. The men rose when we entered, and a waiter pulled out the two remaining chairs at the table. I sat next to the man I didn't know. His white hair was not limited to his head—bristly hairs protruded from his ears.

Melvin met my eyes and held the gaze. Maybe I'd imagined he'd recognized me last time we'd met.

Members of President Fortune's security team stood next to the door we'd entered and guarded the kitchen entrance. A crystal chandelier hung above the table, and mixed green salads waited at each place setting.

"Welcome, ladies," President Fortune said as he raised his wine glass. "I'm so pleased you could both join us." We thanked him before he continued. "I'm delighted to tell you this luncheon has no other purpose than to celebrate and to thank you for all the hard work you're doing to benefit our great nation." He took a sip of wine before returning the glass to the table. "Warden Clark and Ms. Lloyd, I'd like you to meet the newest member of my team, Dr. Colin Gates."

Dr. Ear Hair acknowledged us with a small wave.

"Dr. Gates's research on nanobots caught my attention a month ago. I know he'll be able to help us in our war efforts. But enough of that. Let's enjoy our meal." He snapped his fingers, and two waiters appeared and refilled water glasses.

The waiter serving my side of the table offered wine. "No, thank you. I'm working." However, that didn't stop everyone else, and after the salad course, the waiters replenished everyone's glasses except Melvin's. He'd only been sipping.

Soon, inhibitions were lowered, and President Fortune and Director Spiegel started a dirty joke contest. After each joke, especially the president's, everyone roared with laughter. Martina gazed at President Fortune with shining eyes and rested a hand on his arm. Reminding myself I was Fredrica, I laughed too, but I cringed inwardly. My mother was no saint, but these jokes would've embarrassed her.

Halfway through the main course of salmon, potatoes, and asparagus, I turned to Dr. Gates.

"What kind of research do you do?"

"I'm an epidemiologist."

At least I thought he said *epidemiologist*. His words slurred.

"That's fascinating."

"I'm researching the use of nanobots in public health."

Under the table, I clutched my napkin. Ideas pelted my brain. I had to keep this man talking. "So if we need to keep people healthy, you're our man."

His eyes flicked toward President Fortune, and a lazy grin spread over the doctor's face. "Who said anything about keeping people healthy?"

I forced my expression to brighten with interest. His lowered inhibitions could provide valuable information for the Warriors. "You mean—"

"Dr. Gates," President Fortune said. "Do you have any jokes for us?"

Dr. Gates guffawed and launched into a joke that I tried to ignore but couldn't. Keeping my lunch in my stomach took all the concentration I had.

* * *

After a two-hour lunch, I helped Warden Clark back to the car. Her head lolled against the backseat. "Gonna have to take the afternoon off. Guard, reprogram the car to take me home after you drop Ms. Lloyd off at the prison." She rolled her head toward me. "You were smart not to drink. My head's gonna pay for this big time."

I closed my eyes on the way back and tried to focus on the task I had to finish. Before I left the prison today, I needed to have the interview list complete. After the guard dropped me off and I went through security, another prison guard escorted me back to my office.

Finally, I could open Ben's file without suspicion. I clicked on the blue link that read *Benjamin A. Lagarde*. My eyes skimmed the intelligence test results. He was in the ninety-fifth percentile. I said a prayer of thanks and flipped to his health and psych evals. Ben's health was fine. However, the psych report contained a detail from the doctor that concerned me.

Patient shows unusual religious fervor that could be attributed to mental illness. However, the patient does not display other symptoms associated with mental illness and may benefit from reeducation.

I'd seen similar observations on the evaluations today, but those people had been eliminated due to other factors. I bit my lip and went to Ben's genetic report, praying it would be clear of any major diseases.

I opened the file and stifled a gasp.

CHAPTER 25

Aware of the security cameras, and trying to absorb my disappointment, I willed myself to appear nonchalant. The best way was to think about happy memories with Ben, as I had when I'd fooled the polygraph.

I recalled our first official date.

I was upstairs modeling outfits for my best friend at the time, Tindra. She'd just given her approval to the dress I had on when Melvin knocked on my door and announced Ben's arrival.

I frantically pulled curlers from my hair.

"Chill, girl." Tindra came over and helped me. "I've never seen you this freaked out over a guy before."

I shoved the curlers back on the heating unit. "Ben's different." Ever since he'd worked up the nerve to talk to me, we'd been getting to know each other. There was something special about him.

Tindra rolled her eyes. "Right. A dude is a dude. Remember that, or you'll get yourself in trouble."

I put on strawberry-flavored lip gloss. "What're you talking about?"

"Love. You can't go letting yourself fall in love with a guy. Love is old-fashioned and overrated. It makes you vulnerable."

"That's cynical." But until a few weeks before, when I'd met Ben, I would've agreed.

She shrugged. "It's true."

"Whatever. Hang out as long as you want. I'm out of here."

Ben sat on a bench at the foot of the stairs and stood as soon as he saw me at the top. When I reached the bottom, we hugged.

"You look beautiful," he whispered.

"Thanks." I looked around, expecting to see my mother. "Did my mother come out and meet you?"

"No, just her assistant. He said she's taking a call." Ben held the front door open. "You aren't going to like this part."

I stopped on the porch. "What?"

"Well, your mom's assistant—"

"Melvin."

"Yeah. Melvin said we have to go in one of her cars with Bobby instead of having him follow mine."

My shoulders slumped. Seriously? "She's never done something so ridiculous before." I whirled and started to charge through the door to confront my mother, but Ben stepped in front of the door.

"Let's honor your mother's wishes."

"You're joking, right?" *Honor* her unreasonable wishes? Was he crazy?

Ben's brow wrinkled. "No. I've only lived here a few months. Your mother's probably being careful because she doesn't know anything about me. Have the other guys you've dated always lived in this area?"

"Yes." We'd gone to the same school for years. Ben had recently moved to the Great Lakes Region from the Coastal Plain Region. "Did Melvin tell you that's the reason?"

"I didn't ask." He rested his hand on my arm. "But it'd make sense."

"Yeah, I guess." I sighed. Bobby wasn't that bad. He knew when to keep his mouth shut. "Let's go and forget about it."

Ben took my hand, and we let Bobby chauffeur us to the movie theater. Even though Bobby came into the theater with us, he never said a word when Ben leaned over and kissed me during the middle of the movie.

* * *

It was funny how I'd spent most of my life with my mother being carefully monitored, and now that I'd run away, I hadn't been able to escape being watched. With my emotions in check, I let my mind return to the present and Ben's genetic predisposition for Alzheimer's disease. Though medical science had made great strides in treating the disease, there wasn't a cure, and treatment was expensive.

Ben met the other criteria, and there was no guarantee he'd develop the disease, even if he lived long enough. Yet it would be a strike against him unless I could find a compelling reason to recommend him for Project Harmony.

Ben was a pilot. That might be an option.

I searched the Project Harmony database to see if there was a need for any pilots. On the list of desired occupations, pilot was near the bottom. The government wouldn't want a bunch of citizens with the ability to fly away and escape. In addition, the guide recommended that pilot candidates have commercial airline experience. My heart sank. There had to be something else that would qualify him for Project Harmony and negate his predisposition to Alzheimer's.

Then I remembered a conversation we'd had on our second date and did a quick search of Ben's records in the database while I held my breath. It had to be there. When I found what I was looking for, I was able to breathe again. I made note of a skill exception and added Ben to the list of qualified citizens.

* * *

At six o'clock the next evening, I neared the end of the list. I'd evaluated 284 prisoners, and two remained. Of the 284, only 41 had qualified for Project Harmony. I was finished with last names beginning with *V* and was ready for *W.* I scrolled to look at the two remaining names.

Yeager, Orsen.

Young, Katherine.

My mother wasn't on the list.

Chapter 26

When I arrived at the Union City Federal Detention Center the next morning, Warden Clark, clutching a mug decorated with a picture of a child's face, greeted me.

"Who's the kid?"

She beamed. "My grandson, DeVonte. He's four. Light of my life."

How would she feel if DeVonte grew up to be a prisoner awaiting transfer or execution? When she motioned for me to follow her down the hallway, I dismissed the notion. Fredrica didn't think that way, and I couldn't afford to dwell on thoughts that might reveal themselves in my eyes.

"I'm pleased with the list you finished yesterday," she said. "Officer Ward wants you to complete your interviews of the qualifiers by the end of today."

"Did I have a list of all the prisoners housed here?"

Warden Clark stopped and frowned. "Why?"

"This seems like such a large prison. I thought maybe there were more prisoners someone else was evaluating."

Her face relaxed, and she started walking again. "No. But there are some prisoners we've deemed too dangerous to be a part of

Project Harmony."

"Murderers?" I prayed she'd give me specifics, so I could figure out how to help my mother.

"Something like that." She opened the door of the office where I'd worked yesterday. "You'll have ten minutes with each prisoner. Set a timer to stay on track. Use the interview protocol given in the document. I'll give you five minutes to settle in before I have the guards start bringing prisoners." She breezed out the door.

I sat behind the desk and opened the document that contained the list of prisoners I'd vetted. It was going to be a long day.

* * *

"According to my file, Dr. Willis, you had a dental practice for twenty-five years. Did you enjoy it?" I asked.

Dr. Willis crossed his hairy arms and leaned back in his chair. "Do you mind telling me why I'm here making small talk with a pup who's wet behind the ears?"

I wanted to smile but bristled instead. "I'm sorry. I can't give you details, but you'll be happy to know that you may have an opportunity to use your skills to help others in the future. This interview will help us determine how we can meet your needs as well as the community's needs."

He narrowed his moss-colored eyes. "In other words, the government isn't going to chop my head off because they need someone to fill cavities."

I cringed, but Fredrica was ready with a government-issued answer. "I wouldn't put it quite so crudely."

"Or what? You'll recommend execution?"

"Your relocation has already been recommended. This interview is a formality that'll help us gather information that can help make you comfortable in your new life."

He leaned forward. "What if I'd rather die?"

I folded my hands and rested them on the desk. "Dr. Willis, you're about to squander a wonderful opportunity that could benefit you and your entire family. Now, I suggest we continue."

The family part was a lie that I didn't expect him to believe. He stared at me for a moment before his shoulders drooped.

"Go on."

"Very well. Now, if you will please detail your dietary, exercise, and entertainment preferences, I'll record them for our coordinators."

* * *

As soon as Dr. Willis left, I glanced at the clock. The dentist had put me behind schedule since it had taken nearly twice the allotted time to coax answers from him. The questions appeared innocuous enough, but I was confident the information would be used against the citizens later.

I took a deep breath. Ben was next.

God, you have to help me through this. I can't blow my cover.

The guard's fist rapped against the door before it opened. Like all of the other prisoners I'd interviewed, Ben's legs were shackled, and handcuffs encircled his wrists. He wore a dingy gray jumpsuit with a maroon *R* for rebel emblazoned on his chest and back. The warden separated them from the remainder of the prison's population, not for safety but for deplorable conditions. It would've been better for Ben if he'd murdered someone.

As he sat in the chair in front of my desk, the guard closed the door. They'd shaved Ben's wavy brown hair and his cheeks had hollowed, but prison hadn't extinguished the light in his chocolate eyes.

A lump grew in my throat.

"Benjamin Lagarde?" My voice, even with the alteration device, sounded thick.

"Call me Ben."

"Very well." I stared at the computer screen, attempting to gather my scattered thoughts. "As I'm sure you're aware, the government's been evaluating prisoners."

"Yes."

"After reviewing your test results, your government feels you can best serve your country by participating in a relocation project." I smiled. "This project will allow you to use skills that you've developed to contribute to the greater good of society."

Ben studied me. "I'm not going to be executed?"

"You possess a skill that your government has deemed valuable. Therefore, we expect you to use this skill to serve."

"Ma'am, you do realize I'm in prison for alleged rebel activity, right?"

Ma'am? I looked old enough for him to call me *ma'am*? "I'm aware of that."

"Then why would the government expect that I'll automatically do what it says?"

"Because this is a wonderful opportunity to use your skills to help others."

"Tell me something, Ms....?"

"Lloyd."

"Ms. Lloyd, how many prisoners have willingly gone along with your little relocation program?"

"Everyone so far." A few people like Ben and Dr. Willis had been difficult, but most prisoners realized they were being spared execution. Was Ben willing to die rather than take a chance on being transferred? Didn't he realize his life was important to other people, like his parents, the Emancipation Warriors, and me? Or did he never think of me? The thought pierced my heart.

"I see. And what skill of mine does the government think is so important?"

"According to our databases, you have a photographic memory."

He shrugged. "I'm surprised the government knew. It's not like I've ever made a big deal about it."

"But you participated in a study several years ago in the Coastal Plain Region."

"Oh, yeah. I'd forgotten about that." He nodded. "Was that the day the psychologist took me out of class at school and worked with me?"

I studied the computer screen and looked at the dates. "Were you in seventh grade?"

"Yep. Science class. I didn't realize until that day that everybody couldn't do what I can."

"I'm sure you understand why this makes you exceptional."

"Not really. Lots of people have gifts."

"Whether you understand or not is irrelevant. The government believes you'll be an asset." I glanced at my watch. "We're running low on time, so I need to ask you a few more questions."

I finished asking Ben the list of questions that were similar to the ones I'd asked the others about diet, exercise, and entertainment. Now, I had to try to give Ben a message, so I took a deep breath, charged ahead, and prayed he'd understand.

"Mr. Lagarde, I sense your reluctance, so I want to tell you a quick story. Several years ago when I was in high school, I met this amazing guy. We started talking and eventually planned a date. But when he came to pick me up, I didn't know until we were leaving that my mother had put some stipulations on the date because he was new in town."

Ben stared at me, confusion wrinkling his brow.

I continued. "The stipulations aren't important. But what the guy said to me was. He told me to honor my mother's wishes." I laughed. "Here I was, ready to charge into the house and tell her off, but he asked me to honor the person who was in charge of my well-being even though I didn't like it. Or agree with it."

Understanding dawned in his eyes, but his face remained expressionless.

"I'm sure you see the lesson I learned that day."

"Yes ma'am." The light in his eyes that had been a mere flicker began to blaze. "I see very clearly."

* * *

"We have to fly commercial? At two in the morning?" A few days after completing the interviews, I looked up from the schedule Martina had sent to my MD3. "Why so early?"

Martina sighed. "Ms. Lloyd, do you really think we can safely use government planes to transport slaves? We can't risk the public finding out President Fortune's involved with this deal with the Peacekeepers. That's why we arranged this special flight that leaves when the airport isn't busy."

"I suppose that makes sense." I raised my chin. "But you shouldn't be referring to them as slaves. They're *citizens*."

"Well played." Her tense face relaxed into a smirk. "Now. I went over the list of *citizens* you've assembled. I'm pleased with your work and how you uncovered skills that weren't obvious. Finding out that Lagarde kid has a photographic memory was brilliant. Having a citizen with that potential could be extremely valuable. But I'm removing him from the list."

My heart stopped. "Why?"

"Relax. He's the only one. The rest are fine."

"It doesn't matter." I shrugged. "Did I miss something?"

"No. I have a history with Mr. Lagarde and don't want him around. But you didn't know."

My mind hummed. I had to try something. "Could you send him with another group?" I prayed desperation hadn't crept into my voice. "I'd hate to see his good genes go to waste. Especially if he'd bring a good price."

Martina pursed her lips. "I'll review his file and consider it." She turned to her computer. "Be packed and ready to leave at midnight."

I turned and left her office. *Please, God. Soften Martina's heart. Let her decide to transfer Ben to another group.*

I hoped God was listening, because prayer was Ben's only hope.

Chapter 27

"What do you mean I can't take my courier to Asia?" I glared at Drake's image projected on the wall in my apartment.

"You're undercover. It's not safe."

"I'll be completely on my own."

"God will be with you."

"That's all you've got?" I massaged the bridge of my nose.

He grinned. "Sorry, I'm not being flippant, but if you think about it, that's all you need."

"Sometimes God uses technology."

"True. You do have the Panorama Lens in your eye."

I'd almost forgotten about that. "I told Dr. Park she could put it in, but it creeps me out."

"We can't access it for you because it's activated by your voice."

"How do I send information it records?"

"I don't feel comfortable with you contacting us while you're in Asia. Record the footage and wait until you get back to pass it on."

"Is there enough storage for that?" I asked.

"A petabyte."

I raised my eyebrows. "Impressive."

He gave me more details about the lens, but I couldn't focus on the specs when there were bigger issues to worry about.

"I don't get it," I said. "Why aren't we liberating prisoners at the airport? Why are we letting our own citizens be sold into slavery? How can you be sure people won't be killed?"

"They're scheduled for execution anyway. This is giving them a shot at life."

I threw my hands in the air. "How can you be so callous?"

"*Callous*?" He shook his head. "I thought we were starting to understand each other, but you always think the worst of me."

"I do *not*." Or did I? And if I did, why? Drake liked to give me a hard time, but he'd never been anything but good to me. "I'm sorry. I'm frustrated I can't do more."

"Me too." His frown softened. "Prisoners are coming from all over the country, and we don't know when they're all being transported. Or where they're coming from. If we tip our hand with one rescue, then the government might execute them all. Letting them go to Asia gives us a shot of saving more people, once they're all together."

"What's my objective? I can't pull off a liberation operation by myself."

"Right. Don't even think about it. You're there to gather information that we can use when we do liberate." His fingers brushed his courier.

A few seconds later, my courier buzzed. Drake had sent an access code for the Panorama Lens.

"It's Latin," he said. "Read it, and then say begin."

"*Nec temere, nec timide*. Begin." Strange. A wave glimmered through my vision, and a small red dot appeared in the lower right side of my vision.

"Do you see a red dot?"

"Yeah. Now how do I turn it off?"

"Say the phrase again followed by the word end. To download it to your courier, say 'download' after the word hello. It'll shoot a copy to me."

I obeyed, and a few seconds later, the red light disappeared. Opening a file on my courier, I viewed the recording.

Drake held up his courier. "I've got it."

I shook my head. "So weird."

He grinned. "There's one more thing I need to discuss with you." His face grew serious. "Do not try to rescue Ben."

I bristled. Why did he always make everything about Ben? "You may not have to worry about that." I told Drake what I'd learned from Martina.

"I'm sorry, my dear." He grimaced. "That doesn't sound good."

"But what if they execute him?"

"I'll do everything I can to stop that from happening. We have plans to liberate prisoners here, which could help your mother, but..."

"You're not making promises."

Drake sighed. "I'm not God."

I looked at the floor. "I know." I didn't want to hear him add that God's ways weren't like ours.

"Now if you don't have anything else, I've got to go."

I needed to know how Agatha was. "How's Moonbeam?"

"Fine, or so I hope, since she's working on infiltrating her brother's reeducation center."

"I see." I grinned. "Are you sure there aren't more reasons you're hoping she's fine?"

Drake's eyes gleamed. "Yes. Christian charity."

"You know what I mean."

"I don't know what you mean, so I suggest you ask me directly if there's something you want to know."

I huffed. Why did he always have to be so difficult? "Are you two dating?"

"Why don't you ask her?"

"Because you just said she's undercover on a mission."

"Then I guess you'll have to wait for your answer, because I officially have no comment. Take care, and good luck in Asia." The video screen went dark.

Whatever. I was leaving in a few hours and needed to pack.

* * *

Even though it was nearly one-thirty in the morning, the line for security at Union City International Airport crawled because of multiple steps in the process. Ahead of me, the forty prisoners, drugged to compliance and dressed in street clothes, shuffled forward with their carry-on bags. My interview questions had helped the prison staff know how to distribute the government-provided clothes and toiletries among the prisoners.

I scanned the crowd for Ben and prayed I'd see his face.

Nothing.

When it was my turn to go through the first step, I handed my MD3 to a pudgy woman in a red uniform and stood in front of the retinal scanner suspended from the ceiling. Fredrica Lloyd's ID appeared on the computer screen next to her, along with the words, *identity confirmed.* Thankfully, the nanobots had done their job on my eyes.

The woman grunted, the retinal scanner moved away, and a gate squeaked open, allowing me to pass to the next stage. For a second, I hesitated, glancing over my shoulder in search of Ben. The woman grunted again, and this time it was louder with a note of irritation. I followed the roped path to the women's changing rooms, where I placed my bag on the conveyer belt to be scanned and inspected.

Once it was out of sight, I took a plastic-covered package from a female worker with pink hair and found an empty stall, removed my clothes, and put on the airline-issued travel suit and slippers. Why did they bother with stalls when cameras monitored the entire procedure? Maybe the illusion of privacy mattered to some. The pants and top were navy cotton—the cheap, itchy kind. The slippers were thin socks with a rubber-coated bottom. The benevolent government wouldn't want anyone to slip and fall.

When I'd finished changing, I handed my clothing to Pink Hair who placed it in a bag with a sticker that matched the barcode on my luggage. "Move to step three."

Feeling like an animal being herded, I followed the roped path to the full-body scanner that inspected body cavities using extremely low levels of radiation. The government told us it was safe.

I didn't believe them.

Stepping into the scanner, I held my hands above my head. A few seconds later, I reclaimed my inspected bag and clothes, though I wouldn't be able to change until after the flight arrived in Asia.

As I followed the line of prisoners to our gate, a drunk passenger—one of only a handful of real passengers—stumbled from the bar and ran into a few of the prisoners. Without protesting, the captives lumbered through the gate and down the jet bridge.

Fredrica's MD3 buzzed, and I removed it from my bag. A government message in the middle of the night? I stopped to listen.

"Council of World Peacekeepers Secretary General Navid Zahedi is planning a visit to Union City next week where he will address the Council of Representatives. Secretary General Zahedi hopes to encourage peace on the North American continent and will work with President Fortune on implementing strategies to meet that goal so worldwide harmony can abound."

I put the MD3 away and strode down the jet bridge. If President

Fortune was becoming more open about his relationship with the Peacekeepers, that didn't bode well for the Warriors.

Passengers waited on the plane, but Ben wasn't among them. I found my wide, reclining seat next to Martina in first class, and a flight attendant, whose eyes had the same glassy look as the passengers, smiled and handed me a pillow and blanket.

Surely they hadn't drugged the pilots, but perhaps they had, since the planes could fly themselves. The pilots were on hand in case of mechanical or computer failures.

I squirmed and tried to get comfortable, and when I'd settled, I said a prayer for Ben and my mother. Once I was in Asia, there was nothing else I could do for them. And there'd be nothing the Warriors could do for me.

CHAPTER 28

I stared out the window as the plane descended into Asia the next day, and the ghost city sprawled beneath us in the middle of vast, golden grasslands. A field of wind turbines with spinning blades stood guard to the north. Roads without cars looped the metropolis, and a single road led out. As the plane touched the runway, I scanned the area for an airport, but there was only a wide landing strip and large hangar.

The plane taxied toward the hangar where three busses waited. When the plane stopped, the flight attendants opened the doors, and I followed Martina off the plane and down the metal steps two androids had placed next to the door. A bitter wind penetrated my travel suit. I blinked in the midday sun's brightness.

I gripped the railing, took in my surroundings, and struggled to catch my breath. The hustle and bustle that normally was a part of an airport was absent. Two more androids removed luggage from the plane and transferred it to the busses.

"*Nec temere, nec timide.* Begin," I whispered.

Martina glanced over her shoulder. "What're you whispering about?"

The red light appeared in my vision field. "This whole city is incredible."

"Stop talking to yourself. Is something wrong with you?"

"Yes ma'am. No ma'am."

I followed Martina as she charged toward the busses. She consulted her MD3 and chose the first bus in line.

"Now what?"

She took a seat and motioned for me to sit next to her. "We wait for the androids to finish unloading our luggage. It's marked with our hotel's barcode, so it'll make it to the right place."

"So androids run this place?"

"They handle the menial tasks." She grinned. "Don't worry. You'll have maid service from a real person."

I wasn't worried, but I returned her smile. "Hey, I forgot to ask you earlier. What'd you end up deciding about that Lagarde guy?" My stomach churned.

"I passed that on to a colleague in the Desert and Pacific Region. If he decides he wants Lagarde, my colleague will put him on another flight. As far as I'm concerned, they can kill him. But when I looked at his file, I agreed with your assessment and didn't want his execution reflecting badly on me. So I passed it on to someone objective."

Maybe her argument with Fortune had made her paranoid. *Thank you, God.* There was hope for Ben, but I moved on from the thought and yawned. "Jet lag's so brutal."

She studied her MD3.

In the next few minutes, the rest of the passengers boarded the busses after consulting their newly issued docs.

"Are the prisoners always going to be drugged?"

Martina glanced up from her MD3. "No. The citizens won't be productive under the influence." She chuckled. "Plus, the drug's hypnotic effect is only successful for a short time. People build a tolerance very quickly, so we have to use it judiciously."

"I see."

The droids finished loading luggage. In the distance, our plane recharged in preparation to abandon us here.

The busses drove away from the airport, and they were the only vehicles on the lonely stretch of road that led into the city. Though we were in Asia, signs in English indicated it was Airport Road. How long had they planned to relocate citizens of the United Regions of North America?

When we drew nearer, a metal archway full of intricate designs straddled the road, and in the middle was a huge sign that read, *Welcome to Fortune City.*

Bile rose in my throat. I turned to Martina. "I had no idea this place was going to be named Fortune City."

"It was finalized a couple of days ago. The Peacekeepers insisted on honoring Cleatus. He was thrilled."

I'm sure he was.

The bus rolled past a shopping district similar to the one where I'd eaten lunch a few days earlier in Union City. Except here, there were fully stocked stores without customers. The driver stopped in front of a high rise.

"Attention passengers Dalton, Carson—"

"We'll be getting off at a hotel on the last stop," Martina said. "This is an apartment building."

"—Westwood, Ramirez, Le, and Hodges, we have reached your destination. Please disembark." The passengers filed from the bus, claimed their luggage, and formed a line that snaked out of the building. At the second stop by a high rise, more passengers did the same. Finally, the bus parked next to a ten-story building.

Martina ushered me into the lobby, where elevator music hummed, and at the back of the building, a wall of windows revealed an indoor pool. Lights reflected on the tranquil water, casting eerie silhouettes on the lobby's walls. A lone employee, who wore a black uniform with gold buttons and appeared to be of Chinese descent, stood behind a counter. "*Nín hǎo.*" "Welcome to Ellsworth Hotel. Officers Ward and Lloyd, I am happy you have arrived safely." He offered his formal greeting in Mandarin.

Martina gave me a questioning look, so I took the hint and translated.

She approached the counter, "Thank you."

"*Xiè xiè*," I translated.

The man held up a scanner. "If you will be so kind as to allow me to scan the biochips in your arms, this will give you access to your rooms."

Once again, I translated, and Martina turned her right arm toward the man. A red light flashed.

The man turned to me. "Miss, you are next."

I followed her lead, and he scanned my arm.

"Officer Ward, you will be in room 511. Ms. Lloyd, you will be in room 611." He glanced at his computer screen. "You may proceed to your rooms. Simply allow the scanner at the doors to read your chip, and you will gain access."

I interpreted this for Martina, and we left the lobby.

* * *

After Martina gave me an order to be at her quarters at precisely five o'clock that afternoon, I locked myself into my room, opened my MD3, and chose an application that would scan the room for bugs. It was disguised as a translation app.

A large screen covered the wall opposite the king-sized bed. *Welcome to Ellsworth Hotel, Ms. Lloyd. We hope you enjoy your stay, and we wish to accommodate your every need.* I swiped my hand across the screen, and a menu outlining all the hotel's amenities took its place. Along with the typical room service and spa treatments found in many hotels, pictures of scantily clad men and women, a few of whom looked suspiciously young, gave guests the option of live entertainment.

Disgusted, I turned off the screen and nestled in the cushioned window seat. Surveying the unnatural stillness in the street below, I drew my knees to my chest. No headlights. No taillights. No sirens. The hotel faced what appeared to be a vacant office building.

A lone vehicle passed, and I closed the curtain. Checking the scan's progress on my MD3, I suppressed a chill. The room had three bugs, and a camera behind a mirror stalked my every move. I willed my eyes not to flick to the mirror. Instead, I rose, rummaged in my suitcase, and vowed I'd be changing in the bathroom. I removed my uniform and shook it out before hanging it in the closet.

Since Drake had warned me about not contacting anyone from the Emancipation Warriors, I was alone and without the help of anyone I trusted.

God, please help.

CHAPTER 29

After a nap that was too short, I reported to Martina's room with my camera running. Unlike my standard hotel room, Martina had a suite complete with a kitchenette and a small office area.

"We're taking a tour of the city. Orientation," she said.

I raised my eyebrows. "I'm excited to see it." Did I sound phony?

Martina didn't seem to notice and brushed past me. "Let's go." She led the way out to the street. Twilight enshrouded the city. Streetlights illuminated an executive car parked next to the curb. When we approached, the door slid open and revealed a spacious seat that faced a dashboard of controls. Unlike the cars at home that drove themselves but still utilized an operator, this car clearly needed no one. I hesitated.

"A central transportation system called Flow controls all the vehicles in the city," Martina said.

Once we entered, the door shut, and I breathed in the new leather smell. "Good afternoon, Officer Ward and Ms. Lloyd," a computerized voice said. "Where shall I take you today?"

"Headquarters," Martina said.

"My pleasure. ETA is four minutes and twenty-one seconds." The car glided down the street. We passed two small gray cars that each held one passenger, but the street was otherwise deserted.

Martina pointed to one of the cars. "Those taxis take citizens from their living quarters to their workplaces. Citizens have routines they follow each day, and the revolutionary technology allows them to achieve maximum productivity."

I gulped.

Our car stopped next to a high rise. "We have arrived at your destination. Please exit the vehicle carefully and have a nice evening."

I opened my mouth to say thank you but clamped it shut. Fredrica would *never* thank a computer.

Martina strode into the building's lobby. A massive statue of President Fortune towered over the space. I wanted to vomit. "That's an impressive statue."

"Yes, it is. The president doesn't know. It's supposed to be a surprise for him when he visits. This building is the headquarters for the city's investors."

"I thought the Council of World Peacekeepers owned the city."

"They do. But the investors provide money to maintain the citizens." She led me to an elevator where she scanned her arm. The door opened, and she entered, motioning me forward. "Subway level," she said.

I stepped inside.

"Thank you, Officer Ward," a computerized voice said. "I detect a guest. May I run an identity confirmation scan?"

"Yes."

"Beginning scan."

I leaned against the elevator's mirrored wall. Would the computer recognize me as Fredrica? What if it figured out my real identity?

"I have confirmed the guest's identity as Ms. Fredrica Lloyd. Do you grant Ms. Lloyd temporary access to the subway level?"

"Yes."

The door closed.

"How does this work?" Of course I had a pretty good idea, but Fredrica wouldn't.

"Your biochip is linked to the city through a program called Connect. You have access to more places than a citizen, but not as many as I do." She smirked. "Unless you're with me. Connect can even detect stress in my voice and will block access in case someone tries to use me to access the subway level illegally."

The elevator opened and revealed a platform. A set of tracks ended on my left. To the right, the tracks disappeared into a tunnel. Marble walls surrounded the platform, and several life-size statues of men and women I didn't recognize decorated the room. I walked closer and looked at the engraved placards under each statue. They were men and women on the Council of World Peacekeepers. The largest statue belonged to Secretary General Navid Zahedi.

"This tunnel runs to a secret station fifty miles away where there's a private airport," Martina said. "This allows investors discreet access to the city. The trip takes about twenty minutes, and the train's accommodations are top notch."

"How often do investors visit?"

"Most haven't yet, but there's a celebration that most of them will be coming for in several weeks."

Good to know.

"Let's move on." We returned to the elevator and rode to the one hundredth floor, where we had a 360-degree view of the city. I moved toward the windows and fought a wave of dizziness. A river snaked through the hills and flowed by the airport. The wind turbines' lights blinked in unison like red-eyed demons sent to guard a precious oasis.

Martina stood next to me. "Incredible, isn't it?"

"Yes." I forced myself to sound pleasant, but my dry mouth made it difficult. "Why is this part of Asia so deserted?"

"The Council of World Peacekeepers relocated the people who lived in the area surrounding the city for security reasons, but this area was never densely populated." She cleared her throat. "I have one more thing you need to see."

* * *

One floor down, Martina and I sat in plush theater seats. A droid brought us glasses of seltzer water, and once again, I suppressed the urge to thank it. I took a sip, and my tongue burned from the carbonation.

The lights dimmed. "Good morning, Officer Ward and Ms. Lloyd," a woman's computerized voice said. "Welcome to Fortune City Headquarters. You are about to view an orientation film created to acquaint our investors with Fortune City. Please relax and enjoy the show."

The first half of the movie gave the history of the city and discussed its transfer from Asia to the Council of World Peacekeepers. Then the video described the advanced technological features, such as Connect, Flow, and the Bulwark—the electronic dome that surrounded the city, protecting it from communication with the outside world.

When President Fortune's reptilian face appeared on the screen, I tightened my grip on my water glass. He sat behind a desk. "Welcome to Fortune City. It is my pleasure to partner with you and the Council of World Peacekeepers in bringing about a new metropolis that will advance our global civilization. As investors, you have a unique opportunity to participate in the development of this prototype as a part of Project Harmony. With the success of Fortune City, we'll be able to implement this model throughout the globe, and we'll usher in an era of unprecedented peace."

Yeah. Right.

"Fortune City is now home to some of the best and brightest minds from the United Regions of North America. However, their values and beliefs were hindering the progress of our nation. By reassigning them, we can safely harness their potential and maintain peace and unity in our nation."

I plastered a smirk on my face.

"As investors, you have the unique opportunity to participate in the lives of individual residents by becoming a regulator and helping to provide for their needs. You will make decisions about their health and well-being. Detailed instructions will accompany their profiles, and we trust you will review these in order to better serve Fortune City as a regulator. Thank you for your investment in Fortune City."

The screen went dark, and the theater's lights rose to a soft glow.

I turned to Martina. "Tell me more about regulators."

She stood and glanced at her MD3. "I have a dinner meeting. Go back to your quarters, order room service, and meet me tomorrow morning."

She hurried away, leaving me in the theater.

CHAPTER 30

The next morning, I knocked on Martina's door. "I have a ton of questions."

"They'll have to wait. I have guests you need to meet." She led me into the office area where an Asian woman with tattooed eyebrows waited along with a blonde Caucasian woman wearing false eyelashes. Both of them appeared to be around age thirty, and they wore matching gray uniforms. I smiled at them, but each of the women acknowledged me with a frosty nod.

"Officer Féng and Officer Kozlov, I'd like to introduce you to Fredrica Lloyd, our Mandarin translator and my assistant. She's been helpful in the evaluation and placement of citizens."

I opened my mouth to speak, but Officer Féng spoke in Mandarin. "You will be of good use for us."

That was a weird thing for her to say.

Blinking her bat-wing lashes, Officer Kozlov turned to Martina. "When Russian translator come?" The irritation in her voice was as clear as her Russian accent. Though China and Russia were now united as the Republic of Asia, along with many other nations, cultural and language differences would always make the citizens unique.

"Soon," Martina said. "He arrived on a flight shortly after ours. We could use my MD3 to translate."

The woman glanced at her Chinese counterpart and shook her head as an uncomfortable silence pervaded the room. "Never mind." Officer Kozlov said. "Not needed. My English is good." She crossed her arms, her long scarlet nails contrasting with the gray of her uniform.

If her English was good, then why didn't Martina start the meeting?

I glanced at Martina, but she was staring at the exit. Was something else going on?

A rap on the door distracted my thoughts, and Martina scurried to answer, but instead of the translator, a swarm of men, wearing gray uniforms that matched the women's, shoved Martina aside and marched into the room.

"What's this about?" The color drained from Martina's face.

Officer Kozlov stood. "This morning we receive new orders from your president." She nodded toward the line of soldiers.

Two of them stepped forward and grabbed Martina's arms. Another two headed for me, and I stepped away, but they wrenched my hands behind my back and patted me down until they found my MD3. I fought a wave of nausea.

"President Fortune says you and assistant will be most useful as citizens of Fortune City." Officer Kozlov stepped into Martina's personal space.

Martina's lips settled into a thin line, and her shoulders drooped. Then she squared her shoulders and raised her chin. "This is ridiculous. Let me go!"

I looked Officer Kozlov straight in the eye. "What did we do wrong?"

She smirked. "Many things. Cleatus no longer has use for Martina since he find better woman to take place." Her eyes gleamed.

She must be the new woman.

Officer Kozlov pointed one of her red claws at me. "He has different use for you."

My knees weakened.

"Men will escort you to new living quarters and give new assignments." She turned to me. "You must meet expectations. You bring big price."

"Why would anyone pay a big price for her?" Martina tried to shake the man's hands from her arms, but he tightened his grip. "She's a dorm supervisor I plucked from obscurity."

Officer Kozlov exchanged a glance with Officer Féng, tilted her head, and clicked her tongue. "Cleatus is right. Your arrogance has led to downfall. You should have been more careful."

When the Russian woman took a step toward me, I understood her meaning. Her hand reached below my ear behind my jaw line, and her fingernails dug into my mask. With a flick of her wrist, she jerked it from my face. I yelped, and my face tingled.

Martina scowled and lunged at me, but the man restrained her.

Officer Kozlov wiggled her fingers under my chin, and I spat my mouthpiece into her hand. She didn't even flinch when saliva-covered teeth plopped into her hand. Instead, she tossed them on the table and went to stand inches from Martina's face.

"I have message from Cleatus. He wants to be sure you understand what big breach you make. You recruit rebel. And fugitive. So you must pay."

Martina's eyes bored into me as if the raw hatred shooting from them could cause my death. "Go ahead. Kill her. Kill me. I don't care."

Officer Kozlov smiled. "That is what he told us you would say. He decide it would be best if you live with consequences."

I had a few ideas of what President Fortune might do. My fingers balled into a fist.

"Show her." The Russian woman waved her fingers at the Chinese woman, who walked over to a screen on the wall and brushed her fingers over the surface. When I saw the image on the screen, I turned away as Martina's primal cry ripped through the ghostly city.

CHAPTER 31

Martina continued to scream as the soldiers dragged her from the room. I stared at the floor, afraid I'd catch another glimpse of Martina's little girl with a bullet piercing her forehead.

God, comfort Martina. Help her to know you.

Officer Kozlov stood in front of me. I met her gaze and spoke in a halting whisper. "Why did President Fortune have to kill an innocent little girl?"

"Feel guilty, *Veeveeca*?"

I took a deep breath. "I didn't murder her."

"But she is dead because of what you do to Martina."

"She's dead because Cleatus Fortune is a cruel dictator." I raised my chin. "No mother should ever have to see her child murdered."

Her hand flew to my cheek.

The slap stung, but I refused to flinch. "Did I insult your boyfriend?" She spat in my face and stalked from the room.

I took that as a yes. It felt good to be Vivica again. I wiped my cheek with my shoulder.

Officer Féng approached me and spoke in Mandarin. "We know about your hacking skills, so that is why you are not dead. You will be working on technology with us." She nodded at a soldier behind me. "Take her to her office."

I closed my eyes momentarily. At least I wouldn't be used for entertainment. "How'd you find out about me?"

She walked away.

Two soldiers escorted me to a vehicle that waited by the curb. The car's plain interior contrasted with the luxurious vehicle I'd ridden in hours earlier.

"Where are we going? What will I be doing? Where will I live?"

The men tightened their grip on my arms and stared straight ahead.

The car transported us through the empty streets. We arrived at a high rise, and the men escorted me through the doors and into a small office area just past the entrance.

"Roll up sleeve," one of the men said in a Russian accent as he hit my left arm. I obeyed, and the second man, who was Chinese, readied a syringe.

"What's this for?"

The Chinese man came at my arm with the needle, and a sting bit my arm, spreading warmth through my whole limb.

"This mark you as prisoner," the Russian said. "We track you."

"I already have a biochip." I pointed at my right arm.

"Nanobots. In blood." The Russian patted my head. "We track you."

"So, you're going to take the biochip out?"

"No, no. Biochip stay. Work with nanobots." The Russian grinned and leaned into my personal space. His stale breath made me flinch. "You take biochip out and—" He snapped. "Nanobots kill in thirty seconds. Or less."

The men exchanged glances and laughed.

My entire body felt as if it were aflame.

"Understand?"

"Yes."

"Good. Come."

They guided me out of the room and into an elevator. Was there anyone else in this entire high rise? I watched the numbers increase.

At the twenty-fifth floor, the door pinged and slid aside, revealing a maze of empty cubicles. Both of the men kept their hands on my arms, though it was unnecessary because with the nanobots coursing through my veins, I wouldn't be going anywhere soon.

A row of offices lined the room's perimeter, and they led me to one with an open door. A man with brown hair that skimmed his broad shoulders sat at a computer with his back to the door.

"Mr. Wilkins, we have new worker," the Russian said.

My father turned and met my eyes.

CHAPTER 32

When you lose your father at age four, you don't have solid memories as much as vague impressions that, when pieced together with a great amount of effort, still seem as though they belong in someone else's life. Now I wondered if they *were* from someone else's life. Memories gleaned from books and movies that I'd adopted as my own.

My father had died in a car accident, hadn't he? He certainly hadn't had long hair. Perhaps this man was someone who looked like the father I'd studied in pictures, wondering what kind of person he was. My mother had rarely spoken of him.

If this man was my father, where had he been for thirteen years? But then…I hadn't seen his body. The casket had been closed to everyone. My mother had told me years later the damage was so great from the accident, we'd been advised not to view the body, so we could remember my father the way he'd been in life. Vibrant and strong.

What if the casket had been empty? Or filled with another corpse?

The man before me was thin, the lines on his face pronounced, and his hair was streaked with gray. My skin tingled, and I reached for mental fragments from the day my father had died.

I was playing with the dollhouse my parents had given me for my fourth birthday. My favorite room in the house was the dining room, and I had tiny plates and pieces of clay food that I placed on the table for the family, which consisted of a mother, father, son, and daughter. They even had a dog. A Maltese I named Libby.

I was setting the table for dinner when my mother rushed into my playroom. Her normally perfect makeup was smeared. "Where's Ana?"

My nanny, Ana, came out of my bedroom holding a mound of my cartoon-covered sheets. Her long brown hair was always pulled back in a neat ponytail, and she played dolls with me more than my last nanny, who'd been much older.

"What's wrong?" Ana asked.

"Vivica, come here and sit on the couch with me," my mother said.

I put a turkey in the middle of the dollhouse dining room table, went to the couch, and climbed up beside my mother. She didn't come see me very often during the day.

Ana started to leave.

"Ana, you need to hear this. Please stay." My mother turned to me. "I have some very sad news." She dabbed tears. "Your daddy died in a car crash on the way to work this morning." More tears spilled onto her cheeks.

Ana dropped the sheets and rushed to kneel beside us. She made the sign of the cross while her lips moved in a whispered prayer.

"I won't see him anymore?" I had an idea of what death meant, even if it hadn't reached its cold fingers into my life before that day. I started to tremble, and my mother drew me closer.

"No, darling. We won't. We'll miss him very much, and it's okay to be sad."

Ana held out her hand, and I clasped it. "I'll be here to take care of you, Vivica."

That was true. Ana was nice.

I'd started to cry.

* * *

"Thank you, Vlad, Wang Tao. I'll take care of her from here."

The soldiers released my arms and left the office.

I stared at the man. "Dad?" The word caught in my throat. "How—?"

"They told me you'd be joining me. I'm so sorry." He opened his arms, and I rushed into them.

The memories of his hugs returned the moment he closed his arms around me.

"Why'd you let us think you died? Why're you here? How long have you been here?"

He took a step back. "You look like your mother, Vivibear."

I'd forgotten he'd called me that. Why hadn't I remembered?

"You're beautiful."

"Thanks." I smothered a smile. "But you haven't answered my questions."

He motioned for me to sit in the chair next to him, and I did. "I've been stuck here for thirteen years, developing the technology that makes this place possible."

My heart, which hadn't resumed a normal rhythm, flopped. "Why?

He twisted the gold stud that adorned his left earlobe. I didn't recall him having an earring.

"Long, sad story."

"I have time."

"Which is why we don't need to get into it now."

There was so much to process, and I tried to sort facts. Then something clicked, and my hand flew to my chest. "You're the

Peacemaker, aren't you?"

"I've never cared for that term—a little too super hero—but yeah. I am, and you have the privilege of working with me." He hesitated. "I've been keeping an eye on you all these years...until you disappeared with the rebels."

"Emancipation Warriors."

"What happened to the boy who got you pregnant?" There was no mistaking the edge of irritation in his voice.

"Prison."

"Hmph. Guess he got what he deserved."

"No one deserves that." I glared. "We were both responsible for that wrong. Plus, our wonderful government's pregnancy prevention vaccines didn't work like they were supposed to."

"I know." My father tilted his head. "The vaccines are more about limiting lifespan than preventing pregnancy."

What? "How does that—?"

"I suppose you're in love with him."

I raised my chin. "Yes. What did you mean about—?"

He cleared his throat. "There's plenty of time for catching up, because we're going to be here for the rest of our lives."

My heart dropped. I refused to believe that.

"We're under audio and video surveillance. Every stroke you make on the keyboard is recorded, and don't forget the nanobots they can use against us at any time. The work I do involves the city's security, but I'm perfecting those programs for use around the world." He grimaced. "Fortune and his Peacekeeper goons spared you so we can put our heads together for the good of the world."

His words dripped sarcasm. Obviously, he wasn't too worried about the surveillance.

"My current project is creating a more efficient program to track people who have nanobots in their bloodstreams. They're calling it the Safe Haven Initiative. SHI for short."

I snorted. What a name. I considered what he said. "Right now you and I could just get up and walk away because they don't have the technology to track us?"

"Oh no. They can track you inside this city, and if you try to get out, they'll know. They told you if you remove your biochip, the nanobots will kill you, right?"

"That's true?"

"Yep." His brow furrowed. "You need to sit down? You look like death warmed over."

Every time I thought about the nanobots, it was like I could feel them tickling the inside of my arteries and veins. I set my jaw. "I'm fine. Go on."

"What they need is a more powerful program that can track people over a larger geographic area. The Council of World Peacekeepers wants to use nanobots along with biochips everywhere."

I crossed my arms. "I'd never write a program that'll restrict peoples' freedom."

"You would if you didn't want to be tortured." He refused to meet my eyes. "Besides, the rebels are never going to win the war."

"So I should give up? You don't know how many resources the Warriors have. They can pull off a revolution." I hoped my doubts weren't evident in my tone.

My father chewed his lip. "This war isn't just about the Emancipation Warriors against the United Regions."

"Right." I crossed my arms. "It's about having a government that'll protect the rights of life, liberty, and the pursuit of happiness."

"It's not that simple." He shook his head. "Sure, the rebels are fighting the URNA government, but they're also battling Globalists who believe the Council of World Peacekeepers has sovereignty over every nation on this planet. Secretary General Zahedi's been aggressive with this whole Project Harmony. He's the one who convinced Fortune to sell the prisoners."

I swallowed. "We're fighting the entire world?"

"Something like that. Your little revolution is giving the Peacekeepers the excuse they need to take over North America. Fortune becoming president was by their design, and he's their puppet. Your mother's too much of a Nationalist and has never supported a global agenda, so Fortune did the Peacekeeper's bidding when it became clear that URNA's Council of Representatives was leaning toward confirming your mother's presidential nomination. It's too bad you and the rebels view your own government as the enemy when there are bigger issues."

I thought about the news of the secretary general's visit to URNA, and my heart sank.

My father began typing. "Enough about that. Want to hear the best part about our little city?"

Not really. "I guess."

"Our jobs are only one function in this city. Our personal lives are part of a game. Wealthy investors from all over the world selected us based on profiles, purchased us, and they'll make decisions on our food, clothing, exercise, and entertainment. And personal lives."

"Regulators?"

"Yep. I take it you saw the orientation video."

My mind spun. "That's what the prison interviews were for." A frisson traveled my spine. "To gather information for an interactive prison."

Chapter 33

After we'd finished our conversation, my father had shown me a few more things and then put me to work on learning how Flow, Connect, and the Bulwark operated. Then I could revamp Cater, the meal delivery program, and make it as efficient as the transportation system. I wasn't allowed access to the Safe Haven Initiative.

At least not yet.

Though fear scurried around me, trying to break through my resolve, I refused to let it inside. I was willing to bet the threat of constant monitoring was a bluff, because there were few people qualified enough to recognize and understand everything my father and I were doing.

If only I could be sure I trusted my father. He was disillusioned with the URNA government and the Peacekeepers, but he didn't support the Warriors. His ambivalence scared me.

Whatever was going to happen, I had to buy myself some time to figure out a plan, but since I was required to work, I tried to learn as much as I could about how the city operated. I couldn't improve Cater unless I learned about what already existed.

Once I developed that program, maybe I could help with SHI.

* * *

That evening, when I left the building where I worked with my father, two gray taxis hovered by the curb.

"Good night." My father headed toward the first taxi, and its door slid open. He pointed at the second taxi. "That one will take you to your new apartment."

"Good evening, Vivica Wilkins," a computerized voice said. "Please fasten your seatbelt. We will arrive at your destination in five minutes and thirty-eight seconds."

"Thank you."

Daylight faded while the taxi drove to an apartment building and stopped next to the curb. I stepped out and stared up at the lit building. Pushing through the revolving door, I entered a desolate lobby that contained empty chairs clustered around a screen that displayed my name. I moved closer and swiped the screen.

Proceed to apartment 1053.

I called for the elevator. Why was no one else coming home from work? Regulators must stagger our times to limit interaction.

And to prevent rebellion.

The elevator opened, and I rode to the tenth floor, where I found apartment 1053. Outside the door was a keypad, so I scanned my arm. The door unlocked and revealed a room that belonged in a cheap hotel. I closed the door and cringed when the lock clicked.

A twin bed with a thin flowered bedspread took up most of the space. There was a bathroom near the door. I went to the desk next to the bed. A small screen was mounted on the wall, and a message indicated my dinner of chicken, rice, and broccoli would be delivered in five minutes.

I examined the bathroom and found a small closet of uniforms, undergarments, and shoes in my size. The cabinets contained the toiletries and makeup I used. I thought of the questions I'd asked the prisoners about their preferences, but no one had interviewed me.

How had they known?

I fell on my bed, grabbed the remote control sitting on the nightstand, and turned on the TV. Though I tried all the channels, nothing appeared except a blank green screen. When I tried the menu button, a list of movies and TV shows appeared. They were all choices I would've made for myself.

"Your dinner is ready." The computerized voice startled me. The same message was written on the screen. I glanced at the clock. Dinner was 10 minutes late. No wonder they needed me to create a more efficient system.

The door unlatched, and a tray with a single aluminum container sat on the floor. The hall was empty. I shut the door and blinked away the moisture in my eyes.

It was going to be a long night.

* * *

The next morning, an alarm caused me to leap out of bed and search for the source of the racket. It was the screen above my desk. I punched the button and scowled at the screen in case someone was watching. The alarm faded, and a message appeared in unison with a computerized voice.

`Report to workout room twenty on level one in fifteen minutes.`

"And what if I don't want to, you stupid computer?"

`You will not receive breakfast, and you will be disciplined.`

My eyes widened, and I staggered back. Fleeing to my bathroom, I took a deep breath and dressed in the provided workout clothes. As much as I wanted to rebel, getting disciplined would hinder my plans.

I found workout room twenty and scanned my arm to enter. The area was large enough for a treadmill and drinking fountain. When I stepped inside, the door latched behind me. I pushed on it, and it wouldn't budge. The treadmill was pre-programmed for a forty-five minute workout, and I guessed the door wouldn't release until I'd spent the entire time on the machine.

I started the treadmill and adjusted my pace. Wow. I couldn't believe my regulator wasn't controlling the speed too. After I'd settled into a comfortable jog, I allowed my mind to wander to Ben.

Would he be allowed to travel to Fortune City, or would he be executed? Maybe he was already dead. A lump rose in my throat, and I had to slow my pace when breathing became difficult. I clutched the safety bars. Drake had promised to do his best, but what if that wasn't enough? What if something happened to him too? Or Agatha?

Flashbacks from my last night at the Warehouse overtook my thoughts. The gunshots. The blood. I squeezed my eyes shut, but the memories persisted. I'd never believed what the Warriors were doing was some easy game, but on that night, the war had become too real.

Losing my friends was a possibility. Now that Fortune knew my true identity, my life was in danger, but somehow that didn't seem as important as doing my best to help everyone else. Which meant I needed to stay focused.

When my time was up, the treadmill slowed and then stopped. The door behind me unbolted. Apparently, I was dismissed.

Back in my room, I discovered a chocolate protein bar waiting at my door, and inside, the screen's message told me that a taxi would be ready for me at eight o'clock to escort me to work.

I ate the bar and prepared for my day.

* * *

At 7:59, I stood alone outside my building. The morning was sunny, but a chill lingered in the air. I bounced on my toes and sighed. My breath clouded around me. Where was the taxi?

A few taxis, each containing one passenger, zoomed by, but none of them slowed or stopped for me. Shading my eyes, I glanced down the street. A bus lumbered closer. Were more prisoners arriving? I glanced at my watch—8:01.

The bus parked next to my building, and the new arrivals filed off of the bus and into the building. None of them bothered to survey their surroundings. Inside the lobby, a man and woman dressed in gray uniforms gave each of the prisoners a shot.

A dose of nanobots, no doubt.

The last passenger stepped off. Something about the set of his shoulders caught my attention. I studied the profile and gasped.

Ben.

CHAPTER 34

Knowing I might not get another opportunity, I closed the gap between us. *Thank you, God!*

"Ben!"

He turned slowly and faced me with a glassy-eyed stare.

"Snap out of it." I waved my hand in front of his face. "It's me!"

His expression remained unchanged, so I stood on my tiptoes and kissed him. For a moment, his soft lips were unmoving, but then he responded as he always had.

When I pulled away, he blinked a few times. "Wow." He scrubbed his hands on his face and looked around. "Where are we?" He pulled me into his arms. "Viv, are you okay?"

"Now I am." I rested my head on his shoulder and gave a brief explanation. I lifted my head. "Fortune figured it out. I don't know how. Martina and I are prisoners."

He brushed a stray wisp of my hair aside. "We'll figure this out."

My taxi pulled to the curb. "I have to go."

Ben glanced at the line of prisoners that had diminished. "Me too. We'll talk later." He squeezed my hand and disappeared into the building.

I trudged to my taxi. How long would it be until our paths crossed again?

* * *

I spent the morning fixing Cater while thinking about Ben and fighting a silly grin. Then I caught a break when my father left for a meeting. While he was gone, I learned how the Peacekeepers were monitoring my computer. Once I figured out a way to make it seem like I was working on one thing while I was spying on another, a new realm of possibilities would be available.

It took some tweaking, but I got it. The first item I found was the list of incoming prisoners. Over the next two months, twenty thousand prisoners were scheduled for arrival, and each person had a specific assignment. I searched for Ben's name. Because of his aptitude, intelligence, and photographic memory, Ben was assigned to work in a hospital where he'd take classes and train to become a physician. The Peacekeepers were taking care of the next generation of workers. How thoughtful.

Behind me, the elevator pinged, and I continued working on Cater. My father was back.

"How was your meeting?" I asked, hoping he'd reveal helpful information.

"The usual." His pupils were dilated, which seemed weird in the bright room.

"Are you ever going to tell me how you ended up here?"

"Not today," he mumbled. He shuffled to his computer, and he rested his head in his hands for a moment before starting work.

Something wasn't right.

* * *

Two weeks passed, and I endured the same dull routine interrupted only by two days off, courtesy of my benevolent regulator. One day I was given money and escorted to shops. A week later, I was sent to a movie theater where I had a private screening of a film that had been popular back home. During this entire time, I never once caught a glimpse of Ben.

Finally, after I'd hoped for two weeks for an opportunity to learn more about SHI, my father had another meeting, but just as I was about to start snooping, Officer Kozlov strode through the doorway.

My heart did a somersault, but I greeted her with a respectful nod. Could someone have figured out what I'd done already?

Her brow creased. "Come." She turned toward the elevator, and I had no choice but to follow.

As the door slid closed, the female computerized voice startled me. "Officer Kozlov, I detect a—"

Officer Kozlov's eyes flicked in my direction. "Permission granted," she snapped.

"Thank you," the computer said as the elevator moved upward.

She led me into a massive open space several floors above where my father and I worked. The room boasted an impressive view of Fortune City and the airport. She pointed to a wooden chair arranged in front of a screen. "Sit."

I balanced on the edge of the seat, folded my shaky hands, and prayed she hadn't somehow discovered the extra work I'd been doing. "What can I help you with, ma'am?"

Officer Kozlov snapped her fingers and curtains fell, obstructing the light from the windows. A projector flicked on, and a man's picture appeared on the screen, illuminating the room. Apparently, I wasn't in trouble.

The man was handsome and had perfect teeth, but in spite of a smile, he wore a serious expression in his olive-colored eyes. His sandy hair looked as though it wanted to curl but had been trimmed into partial submission. I guessed he was about twenty. Was he going to be working with my father and me?

"Meet husband." She gestured dramatically toward the screen.

I studied the lines creasing her forehead. He seemed a little young for her. Besides, wasn't she having a fling with President Fortune? "Why do I need to meet your husband?"

"No." She scowled and shook her head. "Your husband. You marry him when he arrives."

A wave of dizziness assaulted me. Surely I'd misunderstood. "Excuse me?"

"What you not understand?" Her bat-wing lashes were getting a work out. "Regulator picked man for you. You will marry and have babies. You fill city."

Fill the city? Did she think I was a rabbit? "How many babies are you expecting?" That detail was the only one I could seem to grasp at the moment.

"As many as regulator decides." She crossed her arms.

More questions began to float to the surface, and most of them I didn't want to face, let alone know the answers to. But the main one thrummed in my mind.

What about Ben?

"This has to be a mistake. I'm seventeen. I'm too young to get married." Not to mention the Posterity Protection and Self-Determination Act in my home country forbade me from carrying a baby to term until I was eighteen. The double standard was absurd.

"No mistake. You will get early start. Lots of babies, remember?"

"What about the pregnancy prevention vaccine?"

"Biochip says it has worn off."

Of course it had. It had been well over a year since I'd had one. Not that it'd worked in the first place. I pointed to the screen. "Why him? What's his name? Does he know he has to marry me? Where is he from? How old is he? What about my work? How will I do my job if I have to raise babies?"

Officer Kozlov held up her hand. "No more talk. Listen."

I bit my tongue.

"You work. We raise babies in nursery." She turned toward the screen. "His name is Nathan Worth, twenty-two years old. He will know you soon. Regulator picked because he is good match for you. Your offspring will be beautiful and intelligent."

The news that we were going to be bred like dogs turned my stomach, but after everything Martina had told me about Project Harmony, I should've seen it coming.

"You will have day off next week for wedding and," she smirked, "short honeymoon to make baby."

I raised my chin. "What if I refuse?"

A throaty laugh bubbled in her throat. "Then we discipline." She tapped her fingers together, and her red claws made a faint clicking noise. "Until you beg for marriage."

The dizziness I'd felt earlier threatened me again. I took a deep breath. I'd have to work harder to find a way out of here before next week.

* * *

Once I was back at work, I tried to focus on the computer screen before me, but everything jumbled and blurred from my tears.

"Dad?"

He glanced up. "What's wrong?"

I sniffed. "They're making me get married."

"Yes, I'm aware, and I'm sorry. This morning, Officer Kozlov told me you'd need a day and a half off." He ran his trembling fingers through his hair.

I swiped away tears with my fingertips. "Don't you think I'm too young? Don't you think I should get to choose?"

He crossed the room and knelt beside me. "Yes. But given your situation, this is what's best for you. Trust me, you don't want—"

I shook my head. "I love Ben. We have to find a way to fix this. Ben and I could get married instead."

He rested his hand on my shoulder. "Peacekeepers' regulations will never allow that."

"Why?"

"The guidelines require marriages between genetically compatible strangers."

And Ben wasn't a stranger. I told my father about my encounter with Ben.

He cleared his throat and frowned. "That was an anomaly that never should've happened. Both Flow and Connect schedule citizens so they avoid running into people they know."

I raised my chin. "God is bigger than the Peacekeepers' stupid computer program. Or some dumb regulator's choice. What if he wants me with Ben?"

"If your god wanted you with Ben, then you'd be a genetic match. And strangers."

"But there's nothing wrong with our son."

"That you know of."

"Whose side are you on?"

His eyes, darkened by large pupils, darted back and forth. "Yours. You need to accept your fate and give Nathan a chance." He hesitated. "Nathan's an excellent choice."

"Why are you getting defensive?"

"I'm not. I'm helping you see reason."

This entire conversation was weird, and his demeanor was bizarre. "Now would be a good time to tell me how you ended up here."

His mouth flattened. "I chose it."

For a second, I sat frozen in place.

Was he one of them?

I shot out of my chair and took a step back. Had he tricked me into believing he was a fellow prisoner when he was working for the government willingly?

"Why?" I whispered.

"It was a chance to get away from your mother. To start over."

My fingernails dug into my palm. Heat rushed to my face. "What about your four-year-old daughter? You abandoned your only child. Do you know what it was like for me?" I closed the gap between us. "Growing up without a dad? At least when I thought you were dead, I knew you couldn't help it!"

He put his hands on my shoulders. "I didn't want to leave you."

I jerked away. "But you did."

"Do you think your mother would've let me have any influence on your life if we'd divorced?"

I looked away. Blaming my mother wasn't fair.

"We couldn't agree on anything," he said.

"So that makes leaving okay?"

"It makes leaving complicated. Sometimes we have to make difficult choices, Vivibear."

Hysterical laughter burst out of my mouth. For someone who said he and my mother didn't agree on anything, he sure sounded like she did whenever she wanted to justify something.

Now I knew what they had in common.

I fled to the elevator. "Don't you dare call me *Vivibear* again!" I jabbed the call button.

"Good afternoon, Vivica Wilkins," the computerized voice said. "I am sorry, but I am unable to transport you from your current floor until your shift ends at 1700."

"Argh!"

Refusing to look at my father, I stomped back to my computer and slumped into my chair. I didn't know how I was going to concentrate on work.

* * *

An hour later, I continued to replay our conversation, and an unanswered question remained, poking me like a stray pebble in my shoe. I stormed to my father's desk and stood next to him until he looked up.

He pushed his chair away from his desk.

"I need to know something," I said.

"We'll see."

I narrowed my eyes. "Why are you so sure Nathan's a good match for me?"

He tilted his head and studied me. "You think I'd let my daughter marry a guy I hadn't vetted?"

"So you picked?" I put my hands on my hips. "How?"

"No. Your regulator picked. Having a husband will distract you and help you be content with your life in Fortune City."

"But I love Ben. Why can't I marry him?"

"I know. But he was never an option for your regulator to choose. Ben's genes are one reason of many. You'll have to get over him."

"They can't make me do this." My voice shook.

"You're a prisoner. You don't have a choice."

I gripped the edge of my desk.

"You think you have everything figured out," he said. "But you don't. You're going to have to trust me when I say this is best for you."

"I'll never trust you!"

He flinched, and his eyes clouded. "Keep your voice down. Do you want guards in here?"

I looked away.

"Nathan is a fine young man. You'll have a lot in common with him. You might even like him better than Ben."

"Never."

"Well, it doesn't matter. Ben will be occupied with his new bride." He paused. "He's getting married tonight."

I lost my grasp on the desk and crumpled to the floor.

CHAPTER 35

My wedding dress was a Chantilly lace ball gown. A row of buttons trailed down my back. I carried lilies, their perfume redolent as I glided down the aisle in the cathedral. A string quartet played Pachelbel's Cannon in D. I drew closer to the altar. My maid of honor, Agatha, waited with a smile along with a pastor and Ben, who beamed proudly at me. The war was over. My son Isaac, with eyes as brown as Ben's, sat in the church with his adoptive parents as well as our families and friends.

A normal life. My happy ending. The dream I was fighting for. Without it, what did I have?

"Vivica!" My father shook me. "Get up. Right now. There's work to do."

I tried to move, but weakness prevailed, and I sagged. "Give me a minute."

He sighed. I rested my cheek on the tile floor and watched my father walk away.

I closed my eyes to fight a vast chasm of darkness full of apparitions, garbed in wedding finery, that swirled and mocked me. They slipped into the abyss along with my hope. This couldn't be happening. I needed to cry. I wanted to sob, but my tears were imprisoned behind a wall of numbness.

I suppose it was foolish for me to have hoped one day Ben and I would be reunited. That we'd have more children and live happily ever after in a free world. That we might be able to visit our son once in a while, not to be his parents, but to see the person he was becoming and let him know he wasn't abandoned. He was wanted.

Loved.

A wave of tears now threatened to engulf me. I couldn't even depend on Drake to come to my rescue. How many times had I counted on him before, and as much as I hated to admit it, he'd been there to take my calls and to listen to me vent.

Even God, with his ways that were supposed to be so much higher and better than mine, had abandoned me. How could he? I'd risked my life to follow him. Was this all a game to him? Did he care at all that I had feelings? Dreams?

Or was he just some big regulator in the sky who had fun manipulating lives?

I clenched my jaw and sat up. Brushing the tears away, I straightened my clothes and walked over to my father.

He surveyed me. "Are you ready to get back to work?"

"Yes." I glared at him.

"Good. I want to see more progress on Cater by tomorrow morning."

* * *

At five o'clock, my father crossed the room, knelt next to my chair, and whispered directly into my ear. "Ben's wedding is at 6:30 tonight at the chapel. The taxi will take you to your apartment building where you'll have five minutes in the lobby before he leaves for his wedding. He'll be waiting when you return home. Understood?"

Tears threatened to spill, but I blinked them away and nodded.

Had my father been responsible for my earlier encounter with Ben?

"You're dismissed." He rested his hand on my shoulder and squeezed it.

I left our office and found my taxi. Though the sun shone, it had sunk behind the skyscrapers, and a purple shadow settled over the city as I got out of the taxi and slipped inside my building.

Ben waited in the lobby next to the screen, and I flew into his arms. I wanted to sob, but I didn't want to spend any of our precious five minutes on tears or my anger at God.

His chocolate eyes looked into mine, and he stroked my cheek. "The artificial pigment in your eyes is fading. Your eyes will be the beautiful aquamarine they're supposed to be soon."

"Is she prettier than me?"

He shook his head. "Ally's pretty, but she's not you."

"I always wanted another chance with you. After I accepted Christ, I thought…"

"I did too." He swallowed. "I guess it's not meant to be."

I clutched the front of his shirt. "How can you give up so easily? We don't have to quit fighting. We could run. Get out of this city. There's a subway. Or you could fly us…" My voice broke in a sob.

"It's too risky." Anguish bled from his eyes. "I have to go through with this."

I dropped my hands and took a step back. "Why? What kind of life can you have here? What about the war? You're giving up?"

"No, there's always hope of a liberation." He ran his fingers through his hair. "I just…" He looked at his feet.

"You what?" Between the two of us, couldn't we think of an escape in the few minutes we had left? "Look at me, Ben."

He met my eyes.

"Have you even met this girl? Do you even know if she's a Christian? You can't marry her if she doesn't share your—"

"She does. That's why she's here." He shifted. "We've met, and I don't understand why this is happening, but it is. Maybe it's God's will."

My chest tightened. "How can you say that?"

"Sometimes God's plan is different than what we want." He buried his face in his hands. "I don't know. I'm sorry." He raised his head. "It's killing me knowing how much this hurts you."

I turned away.

Ben punching me in the stomach would've hurt less than his unwillingness to fight. I fought a scream, took a deep breath, and faced him again.

I wanted to walk away with a tiny bit of pride, so I lifted my chin. "I wish you well. I've always enjoyed spending time with you." Even in my grief, I heard my mother's formal tone echoing in my hollow words. The unexpected thought sidetracked me, and for a moment I stared at the grout lines in the tile before I collected my thoughts and met his gaze. "I never got to tell you, but your son is handsome. He looks like you."

Ben smiled slowly. "What's his name? Is he safe?"

"Isaac. He was safe and healthy when I left him with his new parents. They're good people who'll teach him—" I bit my tongue. I'd started to say *about Jesus*. But I was so over that. "They'll teach him right from wrong."

"I'm glad." He took my hand. "I'll never forget you…and a part of me will always love you."

My tears flowed freely. "I won't forget you either…" I couldn't tell him I loved him. Not now.

He pulled me into a hug and kissed my forehead.

Then he was gone.

* * *

I made my way to my apartment and fell face down on my bed. The sobs I'd held back all afternoon wracked my entire body. My fingers dug into my pillow and, clutching it to my chest, I sat up.

It wasn't fair. I'd trusted God to help me, and he'd betrayed me. Stuck me in a prison. Taken Ben away.

Ruined my life.

I screamed and beat my pillow against the mattress. One. Two. Three times.

A low beep sounded from the communication screen. "Warning. Your biochip indicates your blood pressure is reaching dangerously high levels."

"Shut up!"

Four. Five. Six. Seven times.

"If your blood pressure does not begin to drop within sixty seconds, paramedics will be contacted to come and administer a sedative."

Eight. Nine. Ten. Living didn't matter anymore.

"Forty-five seconds."

Eleven. Twelve. My arms burned. My pace slowed.

Thirteen.

"Thirty seconds."

I dropped the pillow. Lay still. Breathed. In. Out.

I closed my eyes.

"Your blood pressure is dropping. Paramedics will not be contacted."

A new resolve awakened while my body calmed. I wasn't ready to let go of my dream of a happy ending.

But since God had abandoned me, I'd have to figure it out on my own.

CHAPTER 36

"Tell me something." I poured a cup of coffee the next day and faced my father. "Does it ever bother you that you're helping the Peacekeepers take over the world? That you created this awful place?" After my father's willingness to help me yesterday, I needed to understand him—even if I didn't trust him. I took a sip of coffee.

His hand trembled slightly as he tucked his hair behind his ears, and for a moment, pain flickered in his green eyes. "You think you have it all figured out, don't you?" He shook his head. "You may look like your mother, but you're an awful lot like me. Or like I was at your age. Thought I had the answers and knew everything."

"I've never said that."

"You don't have to. You judge me with no idea what my life's been like the last thirteen years."

"Then tell me."

"You know why I grew my hair out?" He pointed to his ear. "Why I have this earring?"

It was a strange question. "Because Mom hates long hair and earrings on men?"

"Right."

I waited for more information, but he walked over to the

kitchenette and poured coffee into his bear-shaped mug. Once again, his hand trembled.

I studied his face. It was flushed. "Are you feeling okay?" Maybe I was being too hard on him.

"I'm fine." He took a deep breath, sat down at his desk, and rested his head in his hands. "Actually, can you get my bottle of pills? I'm getting a headache." He pointed toward the closet opposite his desk. "They're in my bag."

I found a leather messenger bag hanging in the closet next to his coat, and when I dug for the pills, an envelope with *Vivibear* written in large block letters slipped from a book.

He wanted me to find it. Without the cameras noticing.

"Did you find them?"

"Yep." I slipped the envelope up my sleeve and wondered where he'd found paper and an envelope. Then I opened the pill bottle, dumped one in my hand, and closed everything. When I handed him the pill and he took a drink from his bear mug, his eyes searched mine.

"That mug reminds you of me, doesn't it?" I said.

* * *

That night, I slipped into the bathroom, turned on the shower, and slid the envelope out of my sleeve. From my time nosing around Connect, I knew the cameras in the bathrooms were a decoy to make the prisoners believe they were being watched everywhere. My fingers trembled as I opened the letter and sat on the edge of the tub.

> Dear Vivibear,
>
> I know you hate me, but I owe you an explanation. Try to understand my story, even if it doesn't change your feelings.

Your mother's political career was the focus of our family. Whatever feelings she had for me disappeared soon after we married. I don't know if you're aware, but you had two sisters. We were supposed to have triplets. Your mother decided to kill them by selective reduction so she didn't have to inconvenience herself or pay the third child penalty. It wasn't my idea, and she went behind my back.

Things got worse after that. I thought if we moved to Union City so she could advance her political career, our marriage would improve. I even sold my tech firm in the Great Lakes Region. It didn't matter.

When the Council of World Peacekeepers recruited me, I jumped at the chance to develop top-secret technology. They faked my death, and I moved here. It wasn't until I was here that I truly understood the Peacekeepers' intents.

It was too late.

They threatened your life if I didn't cooperate. I complied and became the Peacemaker.

I'm sure you're wondering how I could leave you. The truth is, I'd let your mother have her way for so long that I no longer had a say in your upbringing. I decided it'd be better for you to grow up with no father than a man who'd allowed himself to become his wife's doormat.

When you joined the Warriors, the Peacekeepers' leverage was gone. I refused to work. That's when the torture and medical experiments began.

My "meetings" are sessions to make sure I'm compliant. It's not stopped me from manipulating the city's computer systems here and there. How do you think you ran into Ben the day he arrived?

Now Fortune's head medical guy, Dr. Gates, is using nanobots or something else to influence my mind. It's starting to affect my physical health. I'm sure you've noticed the signs.

I have moments of clarity. And periods of confusion where I can hardly focus on the very systems I created to run this city.

One more thing. Marrying Nathan will be safer for you. If you refuse, they'll torture you, experiment on you, and you may lose your chance of being married permanently. Remember the entertainment choices this city offers. I don't want you to be some despicable man's diversion.

Please marry Nathan. I put him in the program along with other suitable men for your regulator to choose. He's an honorable man who'll protect you.

Love,

Dad

* * *

After a night of tossing and turning, I awoke the next morning knowing what I needed to do. Closing myself in the bathroom once more, I rummaged through my makeup bag, took out the envelope containing my father's letter, and removed my eyeliner.

I didn't have a pen or pencil to write the message I wanted to give my father.

Dad,

I understand.

Love,

Vivibear

Chapter 37

The next day, I slipped the envelope back in my father's bag while pretending to get him more medicine, and after an uneventful day of working on Cater, I returned to my apartment to get ready to meet Nathan for the first time. Early that morning, a message had appeared on my communication screen informing me that we'd have a dinner date tonight. We'd marry in three days.

Someone had brought a dress into my apartment while I was working. Midnight in color, the dress was beaded and shorter than I liked. I put it on and tugged the skirt. Once I would've been proud to flaunt my long legs in a dress like this, but the neckline and hemline seemed immodest. What would Ben think of the dress?

I had an idea, but it didn't matter. He was a married man.

I checked my makeup one last time, grabbed the clutch that matched my ridiculously tall strappy heels, and picked my way downstairs.

My taxi threaded through the city and stopped in front of the restaurant, Imperial Oasis. Like everything else, it was nearly deserted. I stepped out of the taxi and studied my future husband who waited next to the curb.

Nathan took my hand. "You're even prettier than your picture."

He was tall and better looking than his photo. He wore a gray suit with a tie that matched the color of my dress.

"Thank you."

Awkward silence settled between us as he took my arm, and we headed up the steps into the restaurant. He held the door open for me, and we waited for the host while he guided another couple through a sea of empty tables. Even from a distance, I sensed the tension between the man and woman. Another arranged marriage.

The host, garbed in a tuxedo, returned and led us to a private alcove. After pointing out the menu located on a small screen imbedded in the marble table, he left, closing the purple velvet curtain behind him.

I placed a napkin on my lap and swiped through the personalized menu my regulator had created, but the options swam together. My stomach tightened. How would I eat? But I chose beef tenderloin, and entered my order. Clutching the napkin in my lap, I gazed at Nathan.

Though his eyes were serious as his picture had shown, there was a firm kindness in them. He leaned forward and took my hand. "I don't like this any more than you, but I'll be good to you. Since you'll be my wife, I'll honor you and be faithful to you as God intended."

An honorable man. Just like my father had said. I stared at the candle with the holographic flame that danced in the dim light of our private nook.

I imagined Ben saying the same words to the girl he married. Would it be easier for me if Nathan didn't want to acknowledge our marriage as real? If he wanted to get an annulment as soon as possible? Would it give me an excuse to continue to think about Ben?

God would expect me to be faithful to Nathan no matter how the marriage came about, because unless I could stop it, God was going to let it happen.

It wasn't fair.

I pulled my hand away and opened my mouth, knowing I should say something to reassure Nathan, but the words wouldn't come. I took a sip of water. "Thank you."

He sat back in his chair. "How'd you end up here?"

If my lack of commitment disappointed him, his expression didn't show it. I relaxed while I told him my story, beginning with my pregnancy and ending with how joining the Emancipation Warriors had led me here. I even explained the work I was doing with my father. He listened, asking a few questions for clarification.

When I finished, an android delivered our food, and I realized I was hungry because I'd eaten so little since saying good-bye to Ben. "Tell me your story."

"I'm from the Great Plains Region, the part that used to be Canada."

Though Canada, Mexico, and the United States had joined years ago to make the United Regions of North America, most people still specified what country they considered their own.

"My parents have been married for years, and I have two older sisters who enjoyed tormenting me." He grinned. "Anyway, my family was lucky because we had some money, so I went to a private school and played hockey. I started college a few years ago on a hockey scholarship and studied engineering. I met some recruiters for the Warriors. They'd had an eye on me for a while." He cut a piece of prime rib. "I never made any secret that I thought our government had gotten way too intrusive, but I never did anything about it. Then the powers that be started burning unauthorized versions of the Bible, so I read one to see what the kerfuffle was about."

I raised my eyebrows. "Kerfuffle?"

"Gotta love that word. Anyway, after I read the real deal, I accepted Christ as my Savior. Nobody was going to tell me I couldn't tell people about Jesus. So I joined the Warriors." He took a bite.

"And your family?"

"My parents joined and ended up in prison too." He cleared his throat. "I just keep praying they won't be executed."

"I understand." I said a silent prayer for my mother.

"My sisters are married with families. Their husbands are big government supporters."

"Did they turn you in?"

"Nope. My girlfriend did. I still can't believe it because she was so perfect. Well, until… It's like someone knew the type of girl I'd fall for and sent her my direction. So I've wondered if my sisters or brothers-in-law were involved because they introduced me to Kim." His expression hardened. "I was working a mission when the police captured me. Then some officer in prison told me the government was considering me for a special project. I guess I'm good-looking and smart enough not to kill. So I'm here. Ready to procreate and pass on my superior DNA." His eyes twinkled.

I nearly sprayed water before managing to swallow. Nathan chuckled, and I joined. It felt good to laugh.

* * *

A couple of hours later, Nathan and I stood outside Imperial Oasis, waiting for our taxis. When I shivered, he put his arm around me, drawing me into a hug.

"I don't want to be too forward," he whispered directly into my ear. "But there's a device in my coat pocket that'll be more useful to you than me."

I slid my hand into his pocket and grasped an object that felt like a courier. I transferred it to mine while gazing up at him as if I were in love. "How?"

My taxi arrived.

"Some drunk guy bumped into me at the airport and dropped it in my bag after I'd gone through security. I've kept it on me because I didn't want to leave it in my room."

I remembered the man who'd stumbled out of the airport bar prior to my flight to Asia. Had he been warning the prisoners in my group?

"Perfect." I gave Nathan a quick kiss on the cheek and got into my taxi.

* * *

When I arrived at my apartment, I shut myself in the bathroom, turned on the shower, and removed the courier Nathan had given me.

I downloaded every image I'd recorded using Panorama. There was footage of my apartment, my job, the empty city, the zombie prisoners, and every aspect of my restricted life. Including my dog-breeding conversation with Officer Kozlov. There was even some great footage of Martina and me being taken into custody.

I had to figure out a way to get this information to the Warriors. However, the Bulwark blocked all service to the courier, so I'd have to shut the Bulwark down to transmit the information.

After trying to disable the Bulwark, I concluded there was no way I could break through it using the courier alone. I'd have to do it at work tomorrow. I secured the device in the pocket of the uniform I'd wear tomorrow and stepped into the shower to let the water wash away the day's stress.

* * *

The next morning, I reported to work knowing I had to finish Cater, so my father would promote me to SHI. I needed a few minutes to hack into the Bulwark so I could transmit the data on my courier to

Drake, Liam, and Chad. After that, I might not live to tell about it, but at least I wouldn't have given up the fight. Mental images of Ben mocked me, but I ignored them.

At ten o'clock every day, my father went to the restroom, stopped at the coffee maker, and refilled his cup. Today he'd have to make more. At 9:30, I slipped from my desk and poured what remained in the carafe. I dumped in plenty of cream and sugar and returned to my desk before he could notice and ask me to start a second pot.

At 9:59, my father rose from his desk and headed to the restroom. My fingers flew across the keyboard.

The Bulwark proved more difficult to access than I'd guessed, and I wasn't sure I was covering my tracks. Finally, at 10:01, I deactivated the Bulwark and opened Cater. My father would return any second. I removed the courier from my jacket pocket, let it rest on my lap under the desk, and sent the recordings. But the large files slowed the transmission process.

"Vivibear?"

I clutched my desk chair. "Yes?" I tried to sound nonchalant.

"Next time you drink all the coffee, make more."

"Okay, sorry."

The courier was still transmitting data. The coffee pot sputtered. I prayed my father would stay put while it brewed.

"What're you working on?" He peered over my shoulder.

"Cater. Almost done."

He tucked hair behind his ear. "Good deal." He went back to the coffee pot.

I peeked at my courier and started breathing again when I read the words, *transmission complete.* Shoving the courier into my pocket, I enabled the Bulwark as my father returned to his desk.

It wasn't my style to sit back and wait to be rescued, but until I could figure out a way to escape, it was my only option.

Chapter 38

The next day when I opened my makeup case, a folded paper rested on top of my compact. Frowning, I read the handwritten note.

`When you leave, take the middle elevator.`

No signature. Weird. Whoever had written the note knew the cameras in the elevators weren't monitored for sound.

I hurried to get ready and did as the note said. The elevator stopped one floor below mine. The door opened and revealed Martina.

Without a word, she entered and kept her back to me. I clenched my fist.

The door pinged. "Like my demotion?" She pointed to her pink and white dress. "I get to inspect apartments. Make sure they're spotless."

"I wouldn't wish this life on anyone."

"Yet you picked some people who came here."

"My alias picked." I crossed my arms. "Besides, it was part of a bigger mission."

"Whatever makes you feel better." Martina selected the second floor. "Are you working on getting us out of here?"

"If I were, why would I tell you?"

"Because we both need to take down Fortune. He's going to pay for killing my daughter and trapping me in this prison." She stepped closer, pinning me in the elevator's corner. "He has pictures of Eleanor projected onto the communication screens in each of the rooms I inspect."

I gasped and covered my mouth.

"Just to remind me of how I betrayed him."

"I'm so sorry."

"I don't care." She lunged closer, causing me to plaster myself against the elevator wall. "Cleatus is scheduled to visit—"

"I remember. There's a celebration with the regulators and—"

"Shut up." She stuck her finger in my face. "You're going to help me kill him."

I stifled a laugh. "How?"

"What kind of hacker are you if you've been working with daddy and haven't figured out a way around this city's security?" Martina scowled, and her face flushed.

"He's been keeping an eye on me. Besides I—"

"Right. I'm sure he's been paying attention."

"What's that supposed to mean?"

"You haven't noticed?" She laughed. "Daddy dearest's a drug addict."

I reached out my hand and steadied myself on the wall. "He is *not.*"

"What story did he concoct to explain his symptoms?" Her eyes gleamed. "I'd love to hear it."

She was lying. And if she wasn't, my father was an addict because the psychos running this city had turned him into one. "Tell me what you want."

"My biochip restricts me to this building. I need you to hack Connect and give me more access. Like before."

So she could assassinate Fortune. The man was evil, but I was certain murdering him wasn't the answer. I crossed my arms. "There's only so much I can do."

Her brow creased. "Then I'll have to make an anonymous tip that you're up to no good and daddy's too crazy to notice. Maybe you can both join me and inspect rooms. Or there are other jobs I'm sure *you'd* be good at." She leered at me.

My father's warning about the entertainment options in the city lingered in my mind, and my skin tingled. Pretending to help would be better than telling her no. "Fine. I'll look into it."

"Good. I expect you to."

"High expectations are always important."

"You can stick your sarcasm where the sun doesn't shine."

I smirked. "You can do the same with your demands."

The elevator stopped. "Congratulations on your marriage." She winked at me as she exited.

* * *

"I'm ready to present Cater 2.0," I said as soon as I walked into the office.

"Good morning to you too," my father said. "Project it on the screen."

I went to my workstation, started the program, and gave my father a demo. "This should improve efficiency by eighty percent. It'll deliver meals promptly on a regular basis."

He gave me a thumbs up, and I thought of Martina's comments earlier. Today my father's hands were steady, his eyes were clear, and he relaxed in his chair.

"Now what do I work on?"

He tapped his chin. "Take a look at SHI. Start figuring out how it works." He walked over to my computer, scanned his biochip, and opened the program.

Finally.

While I snooped around the Safe Haven Initiative's nanobot program, I considered Martina's request. She'd have to wait. I had more important things to do.

* * *

When my father got up for his morning coffee break, I joined him. "Do you have any advice for me since I'm getting married tomorrow?"

Maybe. I hadn't given up on finding a way out.

Our eyes met, and he took a long drink of coffee before he rested the mug on the counter. His hands remained steady. "Respect each other. It makes life easier. But, I don't think you'll be able to divorce."

My stomach fluttered. How could he be sure? What if my regulator decided differently? "Will you be at my wedding?"

"Absolutely. I've missed so much of your life that I don't want to skip this too." He put his arm around me and smiled.

Perhaps there was hope of us having a normal relationship after all.

* * *

That night I had a message on my communication screen, commanding me to choose a wedding dress. At least my regulator had offered me choices.

I swiped my hand across the screen, perusing all thirty options. None appealed to me. How could they?

Since I'd pictured myself marrying Ben in a lacy ball gown, anything resembling that type of dress was out. I settled on a satin off-the-shoulder mermaid style gown with a beaded bodice. Once I'd picked the dress, the computer gave me veil, shoe, and jewelry options. Something that should've brought joy was meaningless. My days of choosing special occasion dresses with Melvin seemed idyllic compared to this.

I got ready for bed with my mind heavy because of tomorrow's events. I'd work until 2:00 when my captors would whisk me away to a salon where they'd prepare me for the ceremony, courtesy of my generous regulator. My wedding would be at 6:30 tomorrow evening.

Unless I found a way to escape before then.

CHAPTER 39

I awoke on my wedding day with a plan forming in my mind. Martina's request had inspired me to adjust my own biochip access in Connect so I could use the subway to flee. While I waited for my taxi, a frigid wind declared war on my body, and when I arrived at my office, I refused to remove my coat immediately.

"President Fortune's coming today," my father said. "Investors too."

"You mean the slave owners?"

"I hear they prefer the term *regulator*." The tiniest crinkle around his eyes confirmed his amusement. "Anyway. I'll be busy this morning upgrading security. I've already made some changes."

Uh-oh. That could be a disaster for my plan.

"Take a look at SHI and see what improvements you think it needs." He scanned the chip in his arm, giving me access.

I removed my coat and went to work. Later, when he left for a meeting, I looked at the Bulwark and suppressed a groan. What I'd done before to disable it was now impossible because my father had added new features. I squeezed my eyes shut. Had he figured out what I'd done, or was it extra security for the city's guests?

He'd also blocked access to Connect without a scan from an

authorized biochip. My stomach fluttered. I could try hacking it, but would I have enough time?

I bit my lip and tapped my foot. Probably not.

Since I already had access to SHI, I turned my attention to it, to learn what I could.

Prisoners' nanobots contained a unique code that matched our biochips' codes. The bots gave off signals so our jailers could track us all around the city. Additionally, the nanobots monitored our health and could even detect cancerous growths and stop them before they grew out of control. The biochip recorded the tracking and health data the bots detected.

None of this came as a surprise after my tantrum that had caused my blood pressure to spike, but I didn't see how it could help me today. I leaned on my chin and gazed out the window near my cubicle. Heavy clouds hung low on the horizon. The sky appeared as if it could unleash snow, but without a weather forecast, I could only speculate.

When a droid delivered my lunch, I choked down a ham sandwich that was too salty. Maybe the sodium would make the nanobots go crazy. I smirked and continued investigating the relationship between the nanobots and biochips. There had to be something to help me get out of here, but I was running out of time.

Officer Kozlov's threat, along with my father's plea for me to marry Nathan, echoed in my mind. Maybe he was right. I'd always be stuck here and needed to accept it. And Nathan *was* a nice guy. At least, he appeared to be on our one date. But how could I really know?

Should I be like Ben and give up? Accept this nonsense because God was allowing it?

I just couldn't do it.

I pressed forward, but soon my father came and hovered next to my computer. "It's almost time for you to leave."

I glanced at my watch—1:54. I swallowed hard but faked an animated smile. "Will you give me away?"

"Absolutely." He patted me on the shoulder.

When he turned, I had an idea. Why hadn't I thought of it earlier? I hacked into Flow. Fortunately, my father hadn't made changes to this program. My taxi had to be on its way for me now. I put my ID number in the system.

There it was. Empty and only a few blocks away. I entered the taxi's ID number. I could try a manual override, so when I got in, I'd be able to drive it.

1:57.

My fingers flew across the keyboard. There had to be a way.

1:58.

The taxi slid to the curb next to my building. I barely contained a squeal when I figured out how to set the taxi's system to manual.

At exactly 2:00, I left the building, entered the waiting taxi, and pried the panel off of the taxi's console. I grabbed the small knob meant for steering and eased the taxi away from the curb. Pushing the button in the middle of the knob with my thumb, I controlled the vehicle's speed while I steered. Careful not to pass other taxis, I drove toward the edge of the city.

On the horizon, the wind turbines stood stationary, which was odd, considering I'd never seen them motionless.

The taxi jerked to a stop.

"Good afternoon, Vivica Wilkins. I seem to have lost contact with Flow. Please be patient while I recalibrate."

"No!" I jabbed the speed control button, but the vehicle remained immobile.

"Thank you for your patience. We'll now proceed to your scheduled destination."

It had to be my father. Fighting tears, I rested my head against the seat and clenched my fists.

* * *

A white chapel with a steeple and a bell stood on the outskirts of the city. According to the woman who'd done my hair and nails after receiving orders from my regulator, the planners had constructed the chapel for weddings, not religious services. I smoothed my dress while the taxi followed the winding road that led up the hill toward the church. The satiny fabric offered a bit of comfort against the harshness of my circumstances. Was God punishing me for all the bad things I'd done?

This must be what I deserved.

Night had fallen, and snow blanketed the grass. The church bells pealed in celebration. Light poured through stained-glass windows devoid of religious scenes and symbols.

I exited the taxi and blinked away the snowflakes landing on my eyelashes. A low rumble shook the earth. I looked around but saw nothing. Could it be thunder snow? I hadn't seen lightning.

Inside the church, my father, wearing a gray suit, waited. Double doors beckoned us into a dimly lit sanctuary. "You look beautiful, Vivibear."

I wanted to thank him, but the word stuck in my throat. The sound of a low-flying jet caused us both to flinch and glance at the ceiling. Evidently, more prisoners were arriving.

A woman wearing a billowy pink dress handed me a bouquet of white roses before she scuttled down the aisle and took a seat at a baby grand piano at the front. Nathan, handsome in his tuxedo, waited next to the officiant.

When the wedding march began, my father took my arm. Had he not been leading me, I would've remained frozen at the back of the chapel. The aisle was short, and the pews were vacant. Nathan gave me a shaky smile when my father and I stopped in front of the man who would bind two unwilling parties in marriage.

The music faded, and my father stepped away.

"Welcome," he said in flawless English. "We gather this evening for the marriage of Vivica Suzanne Wilkins and Nathan Bradley Worth.

Nathan took my hand. Reassured by his warm, calloused grip, I smiled at him, hoping to ease his nervousness.

"Marriage is not an institution which should be entered into lightly. It must be preserved. Protected. Defended."

Was this guy serious? My shoulders tensed. What a joke.

"Nathan, will you take this woman to be your wedded wife?"

Nathan squeezed my hand. "I will."

"Vivica, will you take this man to be your wedded husband?"

Could I say it? Was this really God's will for me? Everything in me refused to believe that. My tongue stuck to the roof of my mouth. Seconds ticked by. My father cleared his throat.

The chapel lights sputtered.

And died.

Chapter 40

Nathan tightened his grip on my hand and pulled me down the aisle. Behind us, the officiant and my father shouted. With the snow clouds obscuring the light of the moon and stars, oppressive night bled into the chapel.

I tossed my bouquet into a pew and gathered my dress to make running easier, but with the mermaid style, I had to take short, halting strides. "What's going on?"

"Our liberation. Keep moving."

We exited the church, and another jet coming in for a landing whooshed over our heads. A taxi waited next to the church.

"Let's see if we can do a manual override on this thing." Nathan slid into the vehicle.

I told him what I'd tried earlier.

"Anything to escape the old ball and chain, right?" He winked.

"It's not personal." I climbed in and pried off the panel covering the dashboard. "But we have a shot at getting it started if Flow is down from the power outage."

"It's got a battery. Let me try something." Nathan leaned over, ripped a few wires loose, and reconnected them to others.

The taxi lurched forward, and he grabbed the controller knob to steer as my father beat on the window. We fishtailed as we drove away from the church because snow was beginning to stick to the pavement faster than the heating elements in the road could melt it.

"Did you know this was coming?" I asked.

"Sort of. But I didn't know when. There was a message on the courier that guy gave me in the airport, and it said when the lights went out, liberation was coming. I should go to the airport. I deleted it as soon as I read it."

My mind churned with all the possibilities of what was happening. Sudden loss of electricity could mean an electromagnetic pulse. But wouldn't that have disabled the taxi? And what about the planes? It could make the equipment useless. The Emancipation Warriors must've found a way to disable the hydrogen power plant because it would knock out all of the systems that monitored us. But wouldn't the city have a backup power source?

"Do all the prisoners know?"

"I hope so. But you're the only person I've talked to besides the two guys who work in the electronics factory with me." He turned on to the highway that led back into the city. We were the only vehicle on the road.

I rubbed the goose bumps on my arms.

"Take my jacket." He shook it off and handed it to me. The vehicle skidded, and he straightened it.

"Thanks. That's sweet."

"Anything for my girl." He grinned.

We were about a mile from the airport when Nathan growled and slowed the taxi. "Roadblock." Down the road, a few soldiers stood in front of a tank. Nathan did a U-turn and sped away.

They followed with their tank.

"If you have any bright ideas," Nathan said, "now would be the time to speak up."

"How would the taxi do if you took it off road?"

"In the snow?" He glanced in the rearview mirror and laughed. "That's all you've got? We're better off on the road. At least *some* of the snow's melting."

I looked over my shoulder. The tank drew closer. Behind us, an explosion brightened the sky. When I turned to search for the source of the flash, a machine gun fired.

"Get down!"

We crouched on the taxi's floorboard. Above the sounds of a machine gun, a helicopter thwacked. I raised my head in time to see the tank behind us explode.

Nathan sat up and did another U-turn. The taxi trekked back toward the airport and the burning tank, but he had to coax the vehicle through snowy grass. The cab strained, but Nathan maneuvered it back to the pavement until we came to the burning remnants of the roadblock.

The frames of several SUVs dotted the landscape, and charred bodies sprawled on the wet ground. It was obvious who'd been close to the blast and who'd been further from it. I grimaced. These people were our enemies, but they had souls that would live eternally. Were they now experiencing everlasting torment greater than anything they'd planned for us on Earth?

Nathan wove the vehicle through grass and back onto the blacktop, trying to avoid bodies and debris. Smoke seeped into the cab, burning my nostrils. A second explosion, in the direction of the airport, illuminated a helicopter landing on the road in front of us.

CHAPTER 41

Nathan jerked the vehicle to the left to avoid a head-on collision, and we spun before crashing into a smoldering SUV on the side of the road.

The impact jarred my bones and threw me against the window. I moaned.

"Are you okay?" Nathan asked.

I rubbed the shoulder that had taken the blow. "Yeah." Sharp twinges radiated down my arm.

Three armed soldiers jumped from the helicopter and surrounded the taxi. "Get out of the vehicle with your hands up. On your knees. Hands behind your heads."

Nathan and I obeyed. Snow assaulted my eyelashes, and my toes numbed. In the distance, another plane landed. When two male soldiers aimed guns at our chests, my pulse hammered. The female soldier waved a wand over Nathan's body.

She glanced at the handheld machine. "He's fine." One of the men took Nathan by the arm and guided him toward the helicopter.

"What's going on?" Nathan halted. "Where are you taking me?"

The woman waved the wand over my body, and it emitted a series of staccato shrieks.

That couldn't be good.

"The girl's URNA government." The second man grabbed my arms and wrenched them behind my back as he hauled me to my feet. My shoulder protested, and I yelped.

Of course. My biochip registered as Fredrica Lloyd. But the nanobots should've marked me as a prisoner. "It's not what you think. I'm—"

"Shut up." The soldier tightened his grip on my arms.

Nathan took a step toward me, but the man and woman held him back. "Easy there," she said. "Her chip says she works for the government. You know that?"

"If you can explain why my captors arranged a marriage for me with a government employee, I'll listen. But you never told us who *you* are."

They all looked at each other.

"Joint liberation forces," the woman said. "We're North American Emancipation Warriors cooperating with freedom fighters in Europe and Asia to stop the Council of World Peacekeepers."

"Take both of 'em in just to be sure," the man holding my arms said. "Let our superiors decide."

They shoved us into the helicopter, and we took off.

* * *

The airport was as eerily calm as the eye of a hurricane when we landed. Five jumbo jets lingered on the tarmac, and a line of passengers waited to board one of them. Around the airport perimeter, fires blazed as Fortune City's guards tried to keep the prisoners from accessing the airport, but they broke through the barriers with the help of liberation soldiers. Smoke lingered in the air as the soldiers escorted us from the helicopter to the hangar. Nathan's tux jacket hung on my shoulders, but my teeth chattered. The temperature had to be nearing zero.

Battery-powered lamps glowed in the hangar while men and women wearing uniforms milled around. I scanned faces, hoping to see a familiar one.

My eyes met Ben's.

He froze, before recovering and striding toward us. Concern sparked in his eyes. "Vivica, you should be getting on a plane to get out of here."

Seeing him again and knowing he wasn't mine made breathing impossible. My voice quivered as I explained Nathan's and my situation.

"Uncuff them," Ben said to the soldiers. "I'll see that they get on the next plane."

One of the men shook his head. "Not until I hear from your superior."

"Fine. I'll be right back." Ben hurried away.

He returned with Drake a few minutes later. When Drake gave the word, the soldiers released Nathan and me.

"I want to fight," Nathan said.

Drake turned to Ben. "Escort this gentleman to my brother for an assignment."

I started to remove Nathan's jacket.

"Keep it." He gave me a quick hug. "Good luck."

Ben stole a glimpse at me as he led Nathan away. I gave him a half-hearted smile. Drake's brow furrowed as he surveyed me. He appeared as though he wanted to say something, but he set his jaw instead. "You okay?"

"Yeah." I shivered. "Do you think the forced marriages will be annulled?

He stared my wedding dress. "Did you already say I do?"

"No, but—" An explosion thundered, shaking the ground.

"Right now we have other issues to worry about." He put an arm around me and led me toward a makeshift infirmary. "While we get you checked out, tell me everything you know." He pointed to a cot.

"I'm fine."

"Ben told me about the accident. So the doctor's going to make sure." Drake took a blanket from a pile and wrapped it around my shoulders. I climbed onto the cot, and he pulled the curtain.

While we waited for the doctor, I told Drake everything I'd learned about my father and the information Martina had given me about Fortune.

"We knew Fortune would be here, which is why we're liberating now."

"Have they gotten him yet?"

"No, and I can't figure that out. We've got forces all over this city around all the major hotels and apartment buildings, but he's slipped away. Same with Martina."

I thought of the subway station. "There's another way out of the city."

The curtain swished aside and a middle-aged man with a cross tattoo on his forearm poked his head in. "Dr. Myers."

He shook my hand and then conducted the unnecessary exam while Drake waited outside. When Dr. Myers pronounced I'd be fine except for some minor cuts and bruises, Drake handed me a uniform and a pair of shoes before stepping out and closing the curtain. "What's the other way out?" he asked.

"You know, if you hadn't made the doctor do that exam, we could be on our way there now." I tore off the wedding dress.

"What makes you think I'm going to take you?"

"I can be a delicate flower and go get on the plane."

"Really, my dear? That's how you're going to play this?"

"No." I buttoned the shirt and put on the jacket. "Tell me this.

How'd the forces cut the power to this place?"

"They sent a virus into the computers that shut down the hydrogen plant. Then they stopped the river water from flowing in. No water. No hydrogen to harvest. No power. They also put a virus in the backup generator."

"Interesting. How'd they get past the Bulwark?"

"Inside job. We smuggled in couriers that carried the virus. But, it didn't finish uploading until you disabled the Bulwark."

No wonder the transmission had taken so long. I pushed the curtain aside. "I'm ready."

"You never answered my question about the other way out," Drake said.

"There's a subway."

Drake frowned. "We never found a subway."

"Trust me. I've been in there. It's how Fortune got away."

"Can you get back there?"

I grinned. "Absolutely."

* * *

Armed with Diablo 87s, Drake and I took another taxi that Nathan had rewired for us and drove back to the city. The snow continued to accumulate, and the headlights barely cut through the whiteout conditions. At last, we rolled through the streets until we stopped in front of Fortune City Headquarters that Martina had shown me during my orientation. But without electricity, we wouldn't be able to access the subway level by the elevator.

We charged into the deserted lobby. I stopped, closed my eyes, and tried to remember what I'd seen. "I think there's a stairwell at the back of the building."

We found it and took two flights to the lower level where a solid metal door barricaded the way. Next to the door was an electric panel for scanning biochips. Without electricity, we were stuck.

Drake furrowed his brow and studied the door. "I could rig some explosives with the stuff I have in the taxi. See if we can blast it open. Stay here and keep guard." He jogged up the stairs. After the door slammed, I tried to process everything that had happened in the last few hours. But the one thought that replayed in my head was the look Ben had given me. It gave me a surge of hope I didn't have the right to experience.

The door above me opened, and I crouched under the stairwell, praying it was Drake. But two sets of footsteps sounded.

My father walked ahead of a Peacekeeper who pressed a gun to his back. I clapped my hand over my mouth. It was Vlad, the Russian who'd injected my nanobots.

My father stopped next to the door, shined a flashlight on the panel, and removed the outer casing, revealing a lock. Fishing keys from his pocket, he unlocked the door. The man pushed him through and failed to pull it firmly shut behind them.

The door yawned. I sprang from my hiding place and caught the door before it latched. When I slipped into the tunnel, I heard muffled voices. "*Nec temere, nec timide*. Begin," I whispered.

The red light blinked in my vision field.

Lit with battery-powered emergency lights, the tunnel walls consisted of cement blocks. A set of tracks ran along the ground. Ahead, the tunnel opened into the subway station where I'd been with Martina. A sleek, white train sat motionless.

My father and his captor entered the station. With my gun drawn, I tiptoed forward, flattened myself against the wall, and peered around the corner.

"I expect you to find a way to fix this." President Fortune pointed to the train. Two bodyguards hovered next to him.

"How do you expect me to do that without electricity?" My father scowled. "I told you relying on a single hydrogen plant would make us vulnerable. I've said that for years."

"Which is why I insisted on a backup generator."

"Which I gave you," my father snapped. "But they damaged that too."

"Then fix it. Being trapped here in the middle of a battle is not acceptable."

"I sent some men to work on it, but I may need time to undo the virus's damage to the generator."

"How much? I activated the emergency protocol."

My father paled and groaned. "Well, that was brilliant. If the power starts working—"

"We can't let citizens escape."

What was emergency protocol?

"Listen." My father shifted. "I can't fix this problem in a few minutes. It may take a couple of days." He used the back of his hand to wipe sweat from his forehead. "Especially since you people have messed with my mind."

"You don't have a few days." President Fortune's eyes narrowed. "Vlad, kill him now."

My heart somersaulted, and I turned my face away as two shots reverberated in the tunnel. I punched my fist to my mouth to entrap a scream. A third shot rang out.

A fourth.

I peered around the corner and stifled a gasp.

Fortune sprawled on the floor in a pool of blood. Two of his bodyguards and Vlad lay next to him. And my father and Martina stood with guns aimed at each other's chests.

"Give it up, Harrison. You're a pathetic drug addict who'll get the blame for the attack."

"I'm not an addict." The gun wavered. "It's the nanobots."

"You might as well let me kill you. It'll spare you the embarrassment of having your failures become national news."

"*My* failures?" He laughed. "You recruited my rebel daughter."

Martina smirked. "I'll count to three, and we can both lower our weapons. After all, I've just proven we're both on the same side."

"You've proven you're a traitor."

My eyes widened.

"Cleatus betrayed me," Martina hissed.

"Maybe so, but the Peacekeepers won't forgive the loss of their favorite puppet."

"They'll never know if I kill you and make you take the blame." She adjusted her grip on the weapon.

The power surged, and for a moment the lights faded before vanishing.

My father glanced toward the ceiling. "Since Cleatus activated emergency protocol, we're already dead when the electricity comes on."

I had to end this stand-off and figure out what he meant. I needed a diversion. But there was no guarantee it would distract Martina and not my father. It might work the other way.

I tucked my Diablo in my waistband and stepped out of the shadows onto the platform.

I held up my hands. "What's emergency protocol?"

My father and Martina whipped their heads in my direction and then turned back toward each other in unison.

"I told you to give me back my biochip access," Martina said.

She was worried about that right now?

"How are you feeling?" my father asked.

"Fine? Why?"

"Emergency protocol. When the backup generator starts working, SHI will be functional. And the nanobots will get the signal to start attacking our bodies. We'll have about thirty minutes before we start hemorrhaging. Unless we escape this blasted city."

Dizziness flooded me.

"If you have a weapon, take it out and put it on the ground, now." Martina waved her gun in my direction.

"Do what she says," my father said. "She picked off Fortune and his bodyguards." He nodded up at the sniper's nest in the rafters.

I removed the gun from my waistband and put it on the ground in front of me.

"Come with me, Vivica." He shifted back and forth and never managed to meet my eyes. "Your rebellion against the URNA government will be squelched when the Peacekeepers take over. Don't you want to be on their side when they're in power? Think of all the good you could do. We'd make a great team. Finally get to know each other."

It was the brainwashing from the torture. Or nanobots. He didn't really believe this, or he never would've helped me meet with Ben.

"No. I'm going to stay and help destroy this city."

"They have more," he said.

My heart sank. Of course they did.

The lights sputtered, and a blast propelled me forward. My knees smashed into concrete right before my head smacked the ground.

CHAPTER 42

Dust settled around me. I coughed, and my shirt bunched under my back as someone dragged me across ice-cold concrete. I blinked powder from my eyes, and blinding light poured in.

My head ached.

"Let her go." Drake's deep voice boomed through the station.

The pulling stopped. My vision cleared. I lay next to the train, a few feet from the door that led to the train's control panel. My father dropped my arm and edged closer to the train. He aimed his weapon at Drake, who had his Diablo pointed at my father's chest.

"Vivibear, get up and come with me," my father said. "The power's on. If you stay here, you'll die."

"Not if you help me reprogram SHI." I scooted away from the train and closer to Drake. I couldn't let the prisoners die.

"There's not enough time. You need to get away from the signal."

I glanced over my shoulder. Far behind Drake, a damaged statue of a council member swayed. "You're not thinking clearly. Remember what you told me in the letter?"

He hesitated, and his eyes darted back and forth. "No. I'm not confused."

"You said Dr. Gates is using nanobots to control your mind." I rose to my knees.

"That's not true." He guffawed. "They can't do that."

"But you just told Martina—"

"Last chance, Vivibear." He retreated into the train.

"Daddy, don't do this. Don't take their side."

Drake grabbed my elbow and moved me away from the train.

The door slid shut, and it shot out of sight. The vibration on the platform caused the tilting statue to pitch sideways into another statue. Like falling dominoes, they crashed into each other.

We choked and pulled our shirts up over our noses and mouths. My burning eyes fell on Martina, who lay on the platform with bullet holes in her chest. I closed my eyes, momentarily grieving her lost soul. Then, I propelled myself forward, even though my knees ached. "I have to reprogram SHI."

We ran upstairs and out of headquarters to the taxi that Drake maneuvered through the city streets toward the building where I'd worked with my father. The falling snow had slowed, but a few stray flakes lingered. The road's heating elements had finally cleared an adequate path.

Drake handed me his courier. "Call Liam and get the status of the evac."

Liam answered, and I explained emergency protocol. "How many more people?"

"At least five hundred," he said. "But they've made progress with boarding the planes. I'll send a team to try and shut down the backup generator."

"You can't. If I don't have power, I can't reprogram SHI. Besides, the nanobots activated when the power came on. They'll keep using the original command, even if the electricity goes out again. Get the prisoners away from here as fast as you can." I disconnected the call and turned to Drake. "I don't even know if I can do this. I'm starting to get a headache." What if someone was controlling my mind too?

"*We're* going to try. With God's help."

I clenched my trembling fingers around Drake's courier. "Don't you get it? God's forgotten about me. We're on our own."

"Neither of us have ever been on our own." The vehicle skidded, and Drake wrenched it back under control as we entered the city limits. "Where're we going?"

"Turn left. It's half a block ahead."

The vehicle skidded to a stop. We jumped out, ran inside, and took the elevator to the floor where my office had been.

I sat down at a computer. My fingers and toes numbed. Maybe it was the frigid temperature. Or it was my body shutting down.

"We have about fifteen minutes," Drake said.

"About?" No pressure.

"I didn't know I was supposed to set my watch when the power came on."

I took a deep breath, but my hands were shaking, and my thoughts were muddled. I'd never been this confused trying to hack into anything. I tried to access SHI but couldn't get in without a scan from my father's authorized biochip.

"Seven minutes."

"I don't need a hemorrhage countdown!" I closed my eyes momentarily, and when I opened them, I tried to get into Connect.

Without my father's chip, it was useless.

I rested my head in my hands, as if I could entrap my thoughts as they raced in circles. I turned from the computer and faced Drake. "I don't know what to do. I can't think. The nanobots are messing with my brain."

"My dear…I…" He knelt beside me, and my heart turned over at the raw anguish in his blue eyes.

"This isn't your fault." I slid out of the chair and let him wrap his arms around me. "I'm so sorry."

He rested his head on mine. "God," he whispered, "All of us fighting are willing to give our lives. Because freedom means others can share the truth in your word…"

My chest tightened. That was easy for him to pray. He wasn't about to bleed to death. My life wasn't supposed to end this way. I was supposed to be able to hack into the system, reprogram it, save the prisoners, and go on with my life. I should have a chance to tell my mother about how my new faith in Christ had transformed my life.

But had it? My sins were forgiven, and I was on my way to heaven, but had I let God change me? Or was I too busy doing what I wanted?

For my thoughts are not your thoughts, neither are your ways my ways.

Not that verse again. I refocused on Drake's prayer.

"…I pray that you give Vivica an idea, and quickly, Father. If not, we trust in your ways and thoughts because they're higher than our own. Our lives are not our own." He held me tighter.

Goose bumps erupted on my arms.

My life wasn't my own. I'd given it up when I'd decided to follow Christ.

I pulled away from Drake and fell facedown. "God, I'm sorry."

Chapter 43

"God, my life isn't a game to you," I said. "You have a plan, and if that means I die today, I want to be right before I meet you."

"Lord, give us something, please," Drake said.

How much longer until everything faded?

Game. Game. Game.

Why did that word keep floating in my head? When would I slip away? Would it hurt?

Most of what our government does is a big game. You just have to figure out when they're bluffing. Agatha's words from months before reverberated in my mind. I raised my head.

Could I do it? I considered the nanobots. The details I'd learned about SHI. My father's confusion. I had nothing to lose.

I sat up. "Do you have a knife?"

Drake raised his eyebrows. "Yeah."

"Give it to me."

He pulled a knife from his pocket, clicked open the blade, and handed it over.

Gritting my teeth, I sliced my upper arm.

Drake gasped. "What're you doing?"

"Calling their bluff." Tossing the knife aside and fighting a shriek,

I palpated flesh and located my biochip. My blood-coated fingers lost their grip. Flames of pain blazed down my arm.

Drake pushed my hand aside. "It's buried in your muscle. Hold still." He picked up the knife and carved it out.

I screamed.

He tossed the chip aside. I stood, crushed it under my heel, and collapsed.

Nanobots kill in thirty seconds. Or less. The memory of the Russian's laughter mocked me.

Drake removed his coat. Pressing it to my arm, he searched my face.

"I'm betting they lied," I said. "The nanobots won't kill us if we remove the chip because they're totally dependent on the chip."

"How do you know?"

"I don't." I breathed deeply and took the towel from him. "Not for certain. If I'm wrong, I have about twenty seconds." My arm throbbed, overpowering the dull ache permeating my body. "But I was already dead anyway…"

Drake blanched, made a tourniquet from the towel, gathered me in his arms, and raced out the office.

The chill that originated in my toes flourished, taking my body captive. "Remember…you promised…Isaac…"

"You're going to be fine." We were in the stairwell now. Drake's arms were so strong.

"No…weak…" I had about ten seconds.

"You're losing blood."

"My mother…" Darkness stalked my vision field. "I never told her about…" Shadows multiplied.

Brilliant light.

Peace.

CHAPTER 44

My head lolled. I needed to stop its back and forth motion but didn't have the strength to prevent it. I forced my eyes open. I was in a taxi. Before me was the airport, where a jet waited on the tarmac. I rolled my head to the left.

"Drake?"

"They were bluffing."

"But—"

"I contacted Liam. The remaining prisoners removed their chips." He stopped the taxi. "You passed out from blood loss. You may also have a concussion from that blast in the subway."

A soldier approached the taxi and motioned for us to get out. Drake carried me onto the plane where Dr. Myers pointed to a reclining seat. "Soon as we're in the air, I'll stitch you up and give you something for the pain. And a transfusion."

Drake helped a soldier close the door, and the jet began to taxi. I breathed a prayer of thanks as the plane left the ground.

* * *

A few hours later, I awakened from a nap, feeling refreshed. A flight attendant brought me a sandwich, and after eating it, I found it easier to focus. I started thinking of all that we needed to do to stop the Peacekeepers.

When Drake checked on me, I was ready to get back to work. "I have footage of Fortune's assassination." I pointed to my eye. "Can we use it?"

His eyes lit up. "Are you sure you feel like it?"

"Yes."

He led me up a narrow staircase where he knocked on a door. Chad Yeats opened it.

I smiled, glad to see a familiar face. "Nice to see you, Sleuthhound."

"Likewise, Storyteller." He grinned, showing off his dimples.

Drake told him what I had, so Chad stepped aside and let us in. The cabin was set up for work and equipped with the latest technology. Two rows of leather seats faced each other. Tessa and two men I didn't recognize sat working at spacious tables with room for computers.

"You simply must see this footage of Fortune City that just came through." Tessa projected an image from her courier onto the wall behind us.

Massive orange flames besieged tall buildings. In the distance, the wind turbines' red lights winked in chorus, as if giving their approval to the destruction.

"The joint liberation forces that stayed behind blew the city to kingdom come as soon as we cleared airspace," Drake said.

Watching Fortune City meet its fiery demise gave me a surge of adrenaline.

"Chad forwarded us some of the footage you recorded while in Fortune City," Tessa said. "This information, together with the information we already had from our agents, was enough for the European government to authorize a strike on the city with the cooperation of liberation forces."

"And it started with cutting the electricity," I said. Agatha had mentioned Chad's mission had something to do with a hydrogen power plant. At the time, I hadn't given it much thought, but now it made sense.

"Yes. Thanks to some North American and Asian agents, we identified vulnerabilities in the hydrogen power plant that ran Fortune City."

"You know," Chad said, "it's quite strange that the city's power source was so vulnerable."

I smiled as I thought of my father's argument with President Fortune. Perhaps my father had designed the city that way. "It worked out well for us." I thought of something else. "One of my fellow prisoners said something about being told about the power outage before they left North America?"

"Right. The Emancipation Warriors took care to inform as many as they could."

"So what's next?"

"We need you to help us get the truth out about what happened," Chad said.

"And you can use the footage I recorded?"

"Right."

I thought for a moment and then grinned. "I have an idea."

* * *

Chad used the additional footage I'd gathered to create a short documentary that outlined President Fortune's atrocities, starting with the assassination of President Hernandez. I worked on hacking URNA's message system. The material I'd recorded from Fortune City, along with the evidence I'd gathered from Jared Canton, would play a large role in the video that would be shown to every citizen old enough to have the government-issued devices.

Chad looked up from his computer. "When you were working with Agatha, did she ever say anything about me?" His face pleaded for anything I had to offer.

"Why didn't you tell her who you really were? Didn't you know how important trust is to her?"

"They told me to keep it a secret. The fewer people who knew, the better. We couldn't risk the Peacekeepers finding out that countries were cooperating."

"You didn't think she was trustworthy?"

He buried his head in his hands. "That's not it. Not telling her was a way to protect her."

I'd never thought of it that way, and it was likely Agatha hadn't either.

"I need another chance. I want to marry her. Do you think I have a shot?"

I had no idea what was going on between Agatha and Drake, but Chad looked so forlorn I didn't want to steal his hope. I swallowed. "I know she cares about you, but since I haven't seen her…"

His face brightened. "That's all I needed to hear. Thank you." He leaned over to look at my computer screen. "I'll let you get back to work."

I bit my lip and tried to concentrate on my task, but the talk of relationships inflamed the grief I felt over losing Ben. How long would it take me to get over him?

* * *

After the plane landed in Europe, Drake, Chad, and I traveled to an Emancipation Warriors safe house where we spent the night. The next morning, we'd return to North America.

Not long after we'd finished breakfast, there was a knock at the door. When I answered it, a blaze of red tackled me in a hug. "Viv! I'm so glad you're okay."

"Um, Agatha, can't breathe."

She let go and took a step back. "Sorry."

"It's great to see you," I said, but she wasn't paying attention. Her eyes fixed on Chad who shifted awkwardly next to the couch. She hesitated then burst across the room and threw herself into his arms.

Drake and I exchanged glances, but I couldn't read his expression. Was he disappointed?

Drake cleared his throat, and they took a step back.

Color rose in Agatha's cheeks.

"I don't want to break up the reunion," he said, "but we need to get back to North America. Since Chad's coming with us, you'll have the entire flight to catch up."

Agatha squealed as Drake turned and walked out the door.

* * *

I'd wondered if Agatha would leave Chad's side long enough for us to talk, but when we boarded the jet, she took a seat next to me, and Chad sat next to Drake away from the seats where we'd settled. After the plane took off, Agatha told me about her latest mission—liberating the reeducation center where her brother had been held.

"Is he okay?" I asked.

"Yeah. He was glad to see me and wanted to join the Warriors right away, but since they've had a few problems with kids who come right out of the reeducation centers, he had to go through a debriefing program. They need to make sure he's stable and that brainwashing didn't permanently damage him." She studied me. "On the way over here, Drake told me about Ben." She leaned forward. "Viv, I'm so sorry. How are you doing?"

Ben had called me Viv too. I wanted to tell Agatha never to call me that again, but she didn't know better. "I wish I could tell you I'm okay. But I'm not." I flipped the seatbelt flap between my fingers. "I'm past the stage where it's a struggle to breathe every second, but…" Tears pooled in my eyes. "I'm having trouble accepting that we'll never be together."

She clasped my hands. "God has something better than Ben. I know this hurts, but nothing that's happened took God by surprise."

"But it surprised me." I sniffed and blinked back tears.

"That's one of the hardest parts about being a Christian."

Drake cleared his throat. "I'm sorry to interrupt, but we need to have a meeting about our action plan for when we land. Plus, there are some things I need to update you on." He hesitated and handed me a box of reusable tissues. "Unless you don't feel like it. But I need Agatha."

I snatched the box and tossed it on the seat next to me. How much had he heard? Probably a lot if he knew enough to grab an entire box of tissues before approaching me. "I'm fine. Let's get started."

* * *

After we landed and arrived at the safe house near Union City, I went to the kitchen to find something to eat, and as I was unwrapping a granola bar, Drake joined me at the table that faced the living room. I handed him a granola bar, and we ate in silence.

Agatha and Chad sat on the couch with their backs to us. They were deep in a whispered conversation and probably wouldn't even have noticed we were there if they could've seen us. I followed Drake's gaze as he watched them. Our eyes met, and he looked away quickly before he turned, tossed the wrapper in the trash incinerator, and left the kitchen.

I'd seen enough to observe the hurt on his face, and as happy as I was that Agatha and Chad were working through their problems, it annoyed me that she'd led Drake on.

I caught up with him in the hallway and put my hand on his shoulder. The fluorescent lights made him seem older than he was.

"You okay?"

"I should be asking you that question." A wry grin twisted his features. "But, yeah. I'll be fine. It wouldn't have worked between us anyway. Three people in a relationship never works."

I nodded.

"When the other person is in love with someone else, a guy like me doesn't stand a chance. And I'm dumb enough to be drawn to women who are. Or think they are." He closed his eyes briefly. "It's been a long day. I need to get some rest."

As he turned and walked down the hall, I found myself wishing I could comfort him. But I doubted he'd let me if I tried.

Chapter 45

The next morning, I awakened in the room I shared with Agatha. Her bed was empty, even though it was 5:42. She was probably already working out, so I stretched, got dressed, and headed for the exercise room I'd seen the night before. Sure enough, she was already running, so I took the stationary bike next to the treadmill.

"Good morning!" She sounded entirely too chipper for the hour. Even her curls looked perky.

"Morning."

"Chad and I talked last night." Agatha beamed. "He explained how he wanted to protect me by keeping his identity a secret." She held out her left hand, and a small diamond engagement ring sparkled. "We're getting married in a couple of months."

"That's quick. So what about Drake?"

Agatha's smile faded. "That was never meant to be."

"Why? I thought you were perfect for each other."

"Drake and I are good friends, but he was never into me. We even talked about it once."

"How do you know? Did you give him a chance? Or did you lead him on and make him think he had a shot?"

"What's with you this morning? I don't lead guys on." Agatha scowled. "Drake always knew about my feelings for Chad. Give me a little credit. I love Chad. Chad loves me. I had to get over being mad about him lying. Drake understands. In fact, he helped me see reason and suggested I listen to Chad's side."

He did?

She punched the stop button, and the treadmill jerked to a halt. "If you're so concerned about him, why don't you date him yourself?"

"He's too old for me."

"Oh please. That has to be the lamest excuse ever. It's not like he's forty. Besides, you're going to be eighteen in a few months." She dabbed her face with a towel. "You wanted me to end up with Drake so you wouldn't have to deal with your own feelings for him. Now that Chad and I are back together, I'm no longer your buffer." She threw her sweaty towel at me. "Instead, you accuse me of leading him on. Why don't you take a look in the mirror?"

"That's absurd." I threw the towel back at her. "I don't have feelings for Drake, and I've certainly never led him on. He thinks of me like a little sister. Besides, I'm still getting over Ben." I increased the resistance on the bike, and the machine hummed. The burn in my legs eased the fury in my soul.

"Whatever," Agatha said. "Let me know when you're ready to be happy for Chad and me." She stalked out of the room and slammed the door behind her.

"Fine," I yelled.

Agatha could believe whatever she wanted. That didn't make it true.

* * *

When Drake's new sister-in-law, Ophelia, arrived later that morning, he ushered her into the living room where I waited.

"Girl, you and that brother-in-law of mine are gonna have to stop calling on me for disguises. You know, I'm starting to run out of ideas for you two." She grinned and motioned for me to get up. "We've got some serious work to do."

I laughed and gave her a hug. Then we went into the kitchen where she dyed my hair strawberry blonde and applied a new mask she'd made.

Drake came in, leaned against the kitchen counter, and watched as Ophelia put the finishing touches on my disguise. I couldn't read his expression. What was he thinking? Had he overheard my argument with Agatha?

"You're awfully quiet today," Ophelia said.

"Sorry," I muttered. "I'm worried about a lot of things."

"I'm sure it doesn't help that you had a fight with your friend this morning." Drake smirked.

I bristled. "How'd you know about that?"

"My dear, the entire house knew about it. The two of you did nothing to hide it." He crossed his arms. "Thank you for defending me though. That was sweet."

I gritted my teeth. "Any time. I do care about you."

"Yes. I know. You think of me as a brother. And you have nothing to worry about since I think of you as a little sister."

Ophelia removed the cape she'd draped around my shoulders while she fought a grin.

"I'm so glad we're able to clear this up." I walked over to face him. "It'll make things so much less awkward when we have to work together."

"Indeed. I'm glad you remember that. By the way, Agatha always made her feelings for Chad clear to me. Now, I suggest you apologize and then go memorize the information for your new alias."

I turned to leave.

"One more thing, my dear."

"What?" I faced him.

"No one else has enough nerve to tell you this, so I'm going to."

"Drake," Ophelia said, "now isn't the right—"

He glared at Ophelia. "If you're planning on waiting around for Ben to come back to you, I'd strongly advise you to reconsider."

"First of all, I'm not waiting. He's married." I put my hands on my hips. "And since you've never liked Ben, I don't see the need to listen to any advice you have concerning him."

"This has nothing to do with my feelings for Ben and everything to do with you."

"I doubt that, but if you want to believe your intentions are noble, then don't let me stop you."

He took a deep breath. "I spoke with Ben. He has no plans to annul his marriage." In spite of the bluntness of his announcement, I could see he took no pleasure in telling me.

My lungs constricted. Even as I'd tried to accept Ben's marriage, I'd held on to the tiniest hope that maybe someday… "I see." I pulled my new courier from my pocket and held it up. "I assume the details of my new identity are—" I choked back a sob.

Ophelia put an arm around me. "Are you okay?"

I studied Drake's concerned expression. "I'm fine. Thank you for telling me, Drake."

I fled down the hall toward the room I shared with Agatha, but Ophelia's voice caused me to stop.

"…may've been the only one with enough nerve to tell her, but you've got to work on your timing and delivery. Can't you see she's in pain? And don't try to tell me you only care about her as a sister."

I held my breath and clutched the doorframe. First Agatha, and now Ophelia. Heat rose in my cheeks.

"You're right," he said. "My timing stinks. As for my delivery, well if she weren't so irritating…"

Ophelia chuckled.

"But I'll apologize," he said. "I do feel bad for her. Frankly, I'll never figure out why Ben never fought to be with her."

"You may be glad someday that he didn't."

I didn't wait to hear Drake's response, because his comment to Ophelia had cut to the core of what had been bothering me about Ben. He'd made his intentions clear back in Fortune City. He wasn't going to fight for me.

I just hadn't believed him.

Chapter 46

That afternoon, I waited in front of the safe house's TV. Chad's video had been sent to citizens all over the URNA via their docs or MD3s.

The words *Breaking News* appeared on the screen, and I turned up the volume.

"Citizens all over the United Regions of North America are puzzled after a recent video appeared on their government-issued multiphone devices," Jacinda Jackson said. "The video contains shocking allegations that a former Population Management employee, Officer Martina Ward is responsible for the assassination of President Cleatus Fortune. In addition, the video alleges President Fortune played a role in last year's assassination of President Felipe Hernandez and the attempted assassination of imprisoned former governor Genevieve Wilkins."

"The video, which has been credited to a rebel group, claims that President Fortune has been selling political prisoners to wealthy buyers to fund the war against the rebels. These political prisoners allegedly lived in a high-tech prototype city located in the Republic of Asia. Our sources have been unable to confirm this city's existence or the group responsible, but authorities are investigating. The Republic of Asia denies any involvement."

* * *

A week later, the URNA's Council of Representatives issued a pardon to my mother and released her from prison. A week after that, they confirmed her presidential nomination by a narrow margin. By evening, she was sworn in as president in a small ceremony in Union City.

I went to Union City too but stayed at the safe house because I was still a fugitive. I passed the time by helping Agatha plan her wedding. We were experimenting with hairstyles for the wedding one afternoon when a knock on the safe house door interrupted.

I answered, and my eyes widened as Liam, Drake, and Jethro Portner walked into the living room and sat down.

"Sit, Vivica," Jethro said. "We're here for you."

I obeyed. Jethro didn't seem to like me any more than he did when he'd first met me months ago.

I gazed at the men. Had I done something wrong? I folded my hands and placed them on my lap.

"Relax, you're not in trouble," Drake said.

Jethro studied me. "Now that your mama's president, she's made some interesting demands of the Warriors. Well, one in particular."

My mind churned. I wouldn't be here if it didn't have something to do with me. "What's that?"

"She's feeling the pressure from the Council of World Peacekeepers and Secretary General Zahedi to calm this continent down, or they're gonna come in and take over. She's talking about a peace deal between the Warriors and the URNA government. We gotta unite to keep the Globalists from overrunning this country."

Now I had an idea of where this was going and why I was here. I held my breath and braced myself.

"But she won't even begin negotiations unless you agree to come home and live with her again."

I slowly blew out my breath. It was as bad as I'd expected.

"You don't have to do this," Drake said.

The men glared at him.

"Yes. She does." Jethro's snake tattoo twitched. "Think about how many lives could be saved."

Drake jumped out of his chair, and it thumped against the wall. "You promised me you wouldn't put pressure on her." He leaned forward and, for a second, looked as though he were going to hang Jethro using the gold chain around his neck.

Liam rested a hand on Drake's back. "Sit."

Drake shot a nasty look at his brother and muttered something under his breath before he retrieved his chair and followed Liam's orders.

I mustered a small smile for Drake and then turned to Jethro. "What makes you so sure my mother will hold up her end of the bargain if I return? Besides, I'm a fugitive."

"She'll pardon you," Jethro said. "She's feeling pressure from the Peacekeepers and knows URNA's Council of Representatives is divided between Globalists and Nationalists. In fact, 'cause of that, the votes for her pardon and nomination were close. If some of the representatives changed their minds down the road…"

At every turn, it seemed like someone was asking me to sacrifice more than I could possibly imagine.

But my life wasn't my own.

And hadn't I begged God to give me a chance to talk to my mother about salvation? Maybe this was my chance.

"I'll talk to her." But I couldn't make any promises about going home for good.

CHAPTER 47

The next morning, I hesitated outside of the door to my mother's new office in Union City and tapped on the doorframe. She motioned for me to enter. My mother's black Labrador retriever, Commander, leapt from the couch and jumped up to greet me.

"I'm glad to see you're in one piece." She'd arranged her hair in her signature up-do, and as usual her makeup was flawless. But lines on her face had deepened during her ordeal. She'd probably see a doctor soon to remedy the cosmetic problem.

"Same here." I patted Commander's head. "I've been hoping to talk to you about something."

I froze when Melvin walked toward me with open arms.

"What's he doing here?" I hitched my thumb in his direction and backed away.

My mother smiled. "That's a long and fascinating story."

No doubt. "I'd better hear it."

She motioned toward a table that held some carafes that I guessed contained coffee and tea. A silver tray overflowed with a variety of cookies and petit fours. "Let's have a seat. I thought you might be hungry."

I wasn't.

Melvin joined us, and I took a pink petit four decorated with a sugar pansy and nibbled a bite. The cake was dry and too sweet. I tossed it to Commander, who swallowed it in a single gulp.

My mother poured coffee. "First, you need to understand Melvin has never wavered in his loyalty to me. He even assumed Commander's care while I was away."

My mother and Melvin exchanged grins.

"You know how much I love dogs." Melvin rolled his eyes.

She stirred cream into her coffee. "After you gave me the incriminating evidence that proved Fortune planned to assassinate President Hernandez and me, we knew that we had to move forward with caution."

"President Fortune has many allies in the media," Melvin said.

My mother's eyes gleamed. "Melvin is one of the few people I completely trust, so we developed a plan."

"I reported your mother for hiding your pregnancy and for letting you go. I swore my loyalty to Fortune by providing him with the information you'd gotten from Canton. In return for sharing your mother's plans with him for developing the safety and security of our nation, I asked for a place in his administration."

I frowned. "And he bought it?"

"Cleatus was a weak vice president," my mother said. "He'd done very little to actually help President Hernandez. I, however, was well-prepared to assume the presidency. He needed my plans to pull off his sham."

"But how did you know he wouldn't execute you?"

My mother grimaced. "I didn't. And conditions in prison were deplorable. But I trusted Melvin to use his influence. I had to keep my mind on the greater good."

I poured a cup of coffee to have something to do, and while I stirred in some sugar, I pondered my mother's tenacity. I'd never dreamed she'd risk her life to get the presidency back.

I studied Melvin. "You knew I was Fredrica, didn't you?"

"The minute you walked in the room." He took a sip of tea. "But you've been like a daughter to me. I watched you grow up."

"You were the one who told Fortune who I was." My voice quivered. Because of Melvin, Ben had married someone else. I'd almost had to marry a stranger. Then it hit me. "*You* were my regulator."

"Yes." He didn't meet my eyes.

"He had a good reason," my mother said.

"Tell me." I crossed my arms.

"While I was in prison, I overheard rumors of a liberation in some prototype city in Asia. Not only would the Emancipation Warriors liberate detainees in North American prisons, but they'd destroy the city as well. I passed this information on to Melvin."

"Martina informed me the Peacemaker was your father," Melvin said.

I looked at my mother. "Did you know he was alive?"

The grip on her coffee cup tightened. "No. I did not." Her eyes sparked.

"The best chance of helping the liberation was giving you access to your father," Melvin said. "And the control center for Fortune City. So we reported you to Fortune."

"What if that hadn't worked? What if Fortune had decided to kill me?"

"You'd already agreed to put your life in danger when you joined the rebels," Melvin said. "We had to take that risk. All of our lives were in danger. Besides, I'd suggested to Fortune that you're as brilliant as your father and should be spared for the good of the country." He paused. "Lucky for you, he agreed with me instead of Martina. She was already losing her influence because Cleatus was besotted with that Russian woman."

Officer Kozlov. I clutched my coffee cup in my palms to warm my chilled fingers. "Have you heard anything about Dad?" I thought of his moments of clarity and confusion. Was he okay?

"We assume he escaped Fortune City before the Warriors destroyed it," Melvin said. "He's probably in hiding."

"Enough about him," my mother said. "There's more we need to discuss. As I'm sure you've been made aware, I'm willing to make a deal with the Emancipation Warriors because it's the only way to stop the Council of World Peacekeepers and that despicable Secretary General from taking control." She eyed me and stood. "However, there's one stipulation on which I am unwilling to budge. You must agree to come home and live with me. No more running around playing agent or whatever it is you do for the reb—Emancipation Warriors."

"You'd sacrifice the safety of our entire nation if I'm not willing to come home?"

"You'd sacrifice the safety of your nation by refusing?" She put her hands on her hips. "Besides, your Bible says you should obey your mother. Don't you believe in that exclusivist book now?"

Here was my chance. "Yes, and that's what I want to talk to you—"

"I know what it says. I'm simply not interested." She waved her hand. "So honor me, and keep your beliefs to yourself."

Honor. That single word triggered the memory of Ben's words from long ago, and for a moment, the anger over losing him threatened to swallow me, and I closed my eyes. This wasn't going the way I'd hoped.

For my thoughts are not your thoughts.

I couldn't give up on her. Not yet. Which only confirmed my decision. I took a deep breath and opened my eyes. "I'll agree. *If* certain conditions are met."

She raised her eyebrows. "I'll listen."

"Restore religious freedom to every person in this country, and liberate any prisoners who've been incarcerated for their religious beliefs. No more going after exclusivist Christians."

"Their beliefs are divisive."

"You need them on your side."

She pursed her lips. "Go on."

"Abolish the term law and third-child penalty provisions of the Posterity Protection and Self-Determination Act."

She raised her chin, and her eyes met Melvin's.

"This last one's selfish." I hesitated. "Allow me to attend my friend Agatha's wedding in the Caribbean Region. I'm supposed to be her maid of honor."

For a few moments, my mother paced, appearing to weigh my demands. "I suppose I can issue a decree allowing religious freedom. Besides, the majority of Emancipation Warriors are religious nuts. If we're going to be allies, then you're right. I must appease them. However, I can't guarantee how the Council of Representatives will vote regarding PPASDA."

"You're an influential woman who currently has the sympathy of the majority of representatives, governors, and the media due to what you've been through. There'll never be a better time to use your influence for change than right now."

Once more she paced, and then she stopped and faced me. "We have a deal, and you may attend your friend's wedding. With a bodyguard, of course." She extended her hand, and I grasped it. "Welcome home."

CHAPTER 48

One month later…

I handed Agatha her bouquet, and she beamed. "Do you think Chad will like my dress? I wish it could've been new…"

Agatha had borrowed a gown from a friend who was a fellow warrior. Their wedding would be simple, with only a handful of friends and family witnessing the vows. A short reception with cake and punch would follow. It had taken most of Agatha and Chad's savings to afford that, and it was because of generous Warriors in the Caribbean Region that they were able to have their wedding on a beach.

"You look beautiful, and he'll love it."

"Thanks for being here."

"Thank my mother. She's the one who *allowed* me to come." I couldn't keep the resentment from my voice. Outside the door of the little villa on the beach, my new bodyguard, Dane, kept watch.

"Thank you, Genevieve." Agatha grinned and twirled in her dress before stopping and facing me. "Seriously, I know you feel like you've lost, but I believe that God's using you to influence your mother to accomplish his purpose. He already has."

"I hope." My mother had issued a decree granting religious freedom, and Agatha's parents had been released from prison in time to attend her wedding. However, the Council of Representatives had yet to vote on the Posterity Protection and Self-Determination Act.

Agatha squeezed my hand. "I'll pray that you're able to honor her."

My throat thickened. "Thanks. I need it."

"I'm praying about the Ben stuff too."

"It's getting better." I adjusted a hairpin and picked up my own bouquet. "I've accepted his marriage." But all day while we'd prepared for the wedding, memories of Ben had swarmed like unwelcome insects. I bit my lip. "Sometimes it's still so hard…"

"I'm sorry." She hugged me. "God's plans will be even better than the happy ending you imagined." She grabbed my elbow. "Let's go. I'm not keeping Chad waiting any longer."

We stepped into the sunshine, and the sand warmed my toes. In the distance, the wedding guests gathered around a canopy. The gentle breeze and clear sky boosted my hope. I'd discover the ending God had for me.

I'd just have to keep fighting until I found it.

Thank you for reading *The Liberation*, and I hope you enjoyed Vivica's adventure. If you missed the first part of Vivica's journey, then check out *The First Principle.*

Also, I'd really appreciate it if you'd leave a brief review on the website where you purchased the book. It's okay if the review is simply a short reaction to the story. You don't have to write a book report. (I promise not to tell your English teacher.)

If you'd like to be the first to get the scoop about my new releases, sign up for my email list at www.marissashrock.com. I won't share your email address with anyone.

The Liberation Discussion Guide

1. Vivica chooses to fight for her country's freedom, and to do so, she must sacrifice her own dream of a normal life with a happy ending. How far would you be willing to go to fight for your country's freedom? What about your spiritual freedom?

2. As part of her training, Vivica must learn to lie effectively in order to pass a polygraph exam. Are there times when it's morally acceptable to lie? Why or why not?

3. Prior to the liberation at Atlantic Academy, the students attend a government-sponsored circus designed to appease and entertain the masses. What are some specific ways modern entertainment distracts people from the problems in our government today?

4. Vivica discovers her father is still alive, but she is unsure where his loyalties lie. What do you think?

5. Vivica learns that God's ways are very different than our own (Isaiah 55:8-9). How have you experienced this in your own life?

6. Vivica struggles with the idea that God is just one big regulator like her captors. Have you ever experienced similar feelings? When?

7. Ben's marriage is devastating to Vivica. Have you ever been in a situation where a relationship didn't turn out as you had hoped and prayed it would? How did you respond? What did you learn?
8. The story contains futuristic components involving technology, government, and social values. Which of these do you think could happen in the future? Why?
9. Vivica agrees to return to live with her mother. Did her choice surprise you? Why or why not?
10. At the end of the story, Vivica vows to keep fighting for her happy ending. What new challenges do you think she will face?

Credits

Cover Art & Design by Anita B. Carroll at Race-Point.com
Cover Photo by iStock.com/Yuri_Arcurs
Editing by Bethany R. Kaczmarek and Erynn R. Newman at A Little Red Ink
Formatting by Polgarus Studio
Marketing Copy by James L. Rubart at JR2 Marketing & Advertising

www.ingramcontent.com/pod-product-compliance
Lightning Source LLC
LaVergne TN
LVHW020707110826
845149LV00012B/2146

9780996987905